His Jingle Bell Princess

His Jingle Bell Princess

Barbara Dunlop

TULE
PUBLISHING

Chapter One

PRINCESS JASMINE ARCELUS had dressed for confidence this morning. She'd chosen a pair of coal black, textured strappy sandals with heels that gave her an extra three inches. Her business suit was impeccable, a fitted, black skirt with a white silk blouse, topped by a coordinating blazer with trendy leather details. She'd drawn her blonde hair into a loosely braided bun, which was neat without being severe. And her jewelry was subtle, an emerald pendant of her mother's combined with her favorite diamond studs.

In the end, all of it, every bit, had been a colossal waste of time and effort.

Now, as her private plane taxied to a halt at the small airport outside Tucker, Maine, the neatly typed pages of her speech blurred in front of her eyes. The palace communications staff had polished it until it gleamed and she had memorized each sentence, every syllable. Under the watchful eye of her speaking coach, she'd practiced it over and over, experimenting with cadence and expression. She'd nailed it in rehearsal and she'd known she was finally ready.

Then, standing in front of the hand-picked diplomatic

audience in New York City, she'd frozen. The faces had blurred in front of her. A ringing came up in her ears. And she couldn't force her mouth to make a single sound. After several agonizing minutes, the emcee had stepped in and escorted her off stage.

Her failure was an embarrassment to her father, the king, and to the entire country of Vollan.

As the engines of the plane powered down and the jet rolled to a halt on the tarmac, her personal secretary Darren Matzer moved to the seat next to hers.

"It wasn't so bad," he said in a gentle voice.

"It was an unmitigated disaster," Jasmine responded.

There was simply no other description that fit. The sight of her flawless manicure against the crisp pages made her want to throw up. How could someone be so polished on the outside and so terribly flawed underneath?

"I thought the emcee covered up quite smoothly," Darren said.

"Please don't coddle me." When the keynote speaker didn't even open her mouth, there was no way for an emcee to cover up, smoothly or otherwise.

"It was my fault," Darren said with conviction. "We pushed you too hard. We should have recognized you weren't ready."

"But I *was* ready."

There was no possible way to make her any more ready. And that was what had her terrified. How could she become queen if she couldn't even interact with her people?

Darren didn't seem to have another response. Either that or he could sense how close she was to the edge and was afraid to push her over.

She swallowed, moving the conversation on, knowing there was nothing anyone could say that would change what had happened this morning.

"How long is this likely to take?" she asked.

"A maintenance crew is meeting us here. The captain has a charging system warning on the left engine. He expects it'll take about two hours to fix."

Jasmine turned to gaze out the airplane window to the small, utilitarian terminal building at the edge of the runway in Tucker. It was late afternoon, under a thick gloomy sky, with snowflakes wafting down from the low-handing clouds.

She wanted to get airborne again, fly across the Atlantic, and be back home in Vollan, where she could wallow alone in self-pity. Facing her father was going to be brutal. But the sooner she got it over with, the better.

She set aside the speech, closing her eyes against the heavy headache that was forming in the base of her neck.

"I think I'd like to lie down for a while," she told Darren.

His reaction was immediate. "Shall I have Mia turn down the bed?"

"No, thank you. I'll manage." Jasmine came to her feet, smoothing her skirt and checking her hair, still striving for confidence as she started down the wide aisle between the white leather seats and the matching sofa.

Since it was eight hours across the Atlantic, they'd flown in the royal family's largest jet. It offered a private bedroom and a very comfortable bed. She needed some time alone. Some sleep would be even better. She didn't have the slightest idea how she was going to explain her failure to her father.

The King of Vollan had been raised to be stoic not patient, and he was obviously baffled by her phobia. The people of Vollan overwhelmingly supported the royal family. When she was speaking to them, she was speaking to friends. There was no reason in the world for her to be frightened.

But she was. She was terrified at the thought of opening her mouth on a stage.

So far, she and her father been able to hide the fact she couldn't speak in public. But that time was coming to an end. She was heir to the throne and she turned twenty-five next month. On her birthday, she'd be given the title of Princess Royal. With it came a lengthy inaugural speech, where she'd lay out the principles and plans as Princess Royal and that of her eventual reign as queen. It would be followed by a host of public speaking requirements for all the months and years to come.

This trip to New York was her dry run. At a private, diplomatic function, out of the limelight, away from her own people, she'd had a chance to prove her mettle. Truth was, she'd had many chances to prove it in the past, and this was to have been the final effort.

She moved from the main cabin to a narrowed passage that led to the bedroom. There, a gust of cool, fresh air crossed over her face. She paused to inhale, letting the freshness clear her head.

The rear cabin door was opened. Through it, she could see past the tarmac to a cluster of evergreens dappled with snow. It looked like a fairy tale Christmas forest—crisp, clean, and simple.

A narrow, metal staircase led down to the runway. From there, she could walk to the woods, disappear into them for just a little while. She wished it was possible. But it was freezing outside, the wind and snow were picking up, and she definitely wasn't dressed for a winter stroll.

She gave up on the fantasy, focusing on the bedroom instead. But then she caught sight of a cupboard, its door slightly ajar. A closer look revealed a navy blue work jacket and a pair of lined, rubber boots.

She made up her mind. Fresh air might clear her headache, and a brisk walk would help her sleep. And there was nobody out there in that Christmas tree forest to pity or judge her. She needed that right now. She needed it badly.

She shrugged into the jacket, popped up the hood, and stepped into the boots.

The corrugated metal stairway felt rickety beneath her feet. It was narrower than the one that led to the front cabin door, and a wind was gusting against it, making it rattle and sway. But she held onto the rails and easily made it to the bottom, stepping onto solid ground. She felt like she could breathe for the first time in a week.

The boots were big and clunky, but the jacket was warm, the sleeves coming down to cover her hands. The snowflakes were big, tapping against her face and melting on her cheeks and nose. Her knees were bare and felt the cold, but she wasn't going to let that stop her. It wasn't very far to the edge of the woods.

As she walked, the speech played through her mind, and she began reciting it out loud. There were few planes on the tarmac, none of them running. Only a couple of trucks and a few members of the ground crew were on the runway apron. They were working near the terminal building, which was fading in the gloom. Nobody was close enough to overhear her and her voice rose with confidence.

She nailed every beat. And by the time she made it to the fence, she was kicking herself all over again. She grasped the chain link, but quickly pulled her hands back from the sting of the cold metal. The trees were only twenty feet away. She was almost there.

She glanced up and down the fence line, spying a gate.

She expected to find it locked. But it was slightly ajar, blocked open by the large stone. Since there was no one around to object, she slipped through the opening.

SAM CUTLER SWUNG his pickup truck to the curb at the corner of Main and Pine Tree Avenue, grateful to see the end of another emotionally grueling day. As the holidays crept closer, he felt a rising sense of anxiety, even panic at the thought of smiling his way through Tucker's annual celebrations.

Inside the truck's cab, his nine-year-old daughter Amelia bounced to the middle of the bench seat to make room, while her twin sister Sophie glided down the steps of the community center in her white down-filled coat with the fuzzy fur collar. Her cheeks were flushed from the exertion of her dance class, and there was a smile on her face.

"Hi, Sophie," Amelia said.

Sophie climbed gracefully into the cab, shutting the door and reaching for her seatbelt.

"Did you do it?" Sophie asked her sister as she buckled up.

"I did it," Amelia sang out. "I hit the bull's-eye."

Sophie raised her palm to give her sister a high five.

Amelia's archery lessons were in stark contrast to Sophie's dance, but the girls had always taken their differences in stride.

"Can we cut the tree tonight?" asked Amelia. "Can we, Daddy?"

"Oh, can we?" asked Sophie, all but holding her breath in anticipation.

A lump formed in Sam's throat, but he swallowed it

down. He'd been hoping for a few more days before they brought a Christmas into the house.

"How are we going to cut a Christmas tree in the dark?" he asked.

"Mr. Harry says he's lighting up the Christmas tree forest tonight," Amelia said. "And if we go right away, we'll get one of the first picks."

The Christmas tree forest had been a tradition in Tucker, Maine for nearly fifty years. Every Christmas, families cut a tree from a special section of woods on Bert Harry's hobby farm. Then every spring, the school children planted new trees. The result was a constant supply of trees the right age and size for harvesting.

Sam knew a tree was inevitable, but he hadn't had time to mentally prepare himself for the ordeal. Every light, every ornament, every string of tinsel would be a stark reminder of his wife Kara and the horrible accident two years ago.

He was happy his daughters were recovering, finding the joy in Christmas once again. He told himself to follow their example. He knew he could be more resilient if he put his mind to it. Tragedies happened and people moved on. There was no other choice.

"Sure," he said, forcing some enthusiasm into his voice. "But I called ahead and ordered pizza. So let's get changed and eat first."

"Goody!" Both girls squealed in unison.

Sam drove a few more blocks before pulling the pickup

truck into the driveway of his mother-in-law's historic mansion. He was renovating his own house and they were temporarily staying with Belle until it was done.

Truth was that temporarily had turned into more months than he cared to count. But his mother-in-law seemed happy to have them there, so he'd stopped worrying about the timeline.

"I want a bushy one," Sophie said as she slid to the ground.

"I want a tall one," Amelia said, closing the truck door. "Daddy, can we make gingerbread for decorations?"

The last thing Sam wanted was a house filled with sweet Christmas smells, but he couldn't refuse them their treasured traditions. "We'll have to ask Grandma about that."

"You ate all the peppermints last time," Sophie said to her sister as they made their way up the walk.

"You ate the jellies," Amelia responded.

The good natured argument brought back memories of Kara in the kitchen, the girls, barely six at the time, encased in big aprons, covered in flour, licking green icing from a spoon. Like most kids, they each had a sweet tooth. Sam and Kara normally tried to keep their daughter's candy consumption to a minimum. But when Christmas rolled around, they pretty much gave up.

He lifted his tool belt from the pickup box, following the girls in through the side door of the old colonial. Belle had purchased the aging mansion when Sam was a teenager and already dating Kara. Helping her fix it up had triggered his first interest in carpentry.

It was a stately brick house with a fresh airy interior. The rooms were large, the walls white, and the arched windows let in plenty of sunlight. He was always careful of the ivory marble floors, removing his work boots in the mud room. Although the front entrance and the living room were opulent, the kitchen was more rustic. The girls' room was a cozy blend of creams and pastels.

He could tell by the quiet, that Belle wasn't yet home. The girls kicked off their boots and raced for the den to watch the next episode of their favorite comedy series. He knew they were banking on Belle being late. If she arrived before the pizza, they'd have to eat at the table in the kitchen. But if Belle wasn't around, especially on nights when he was feeling particularly drained, Sam sometimes let them have their pizza in front of the television.

Tonight was one of those nights. Like his daughters, he was secretly hoping his mother-in-law would be late.

The pizza arrived before Belle. And though Sam had little interest in the rollicking adventures of a group of teenage girlfriends in the California suburbs, he watched the program with his daughters and devoured several slices.

"Do you think I could get a pair of glasses like Nina's?" Amelia asked Sam as she finished a second slice of pizza. Nina was a main character on the show.

"You don't need glasses," he said.

"I could get some with clear lenses. They'd look really cool. Plus, it would help people tell me and Sophie apart."

"Do people have trouble telling you apart?" he asked, knowing their friends and family had no trouble at all.

If nothing else, their clothes were a dead giveaway. Sophie liked color and flash, while Amelia went for earth tones and neutrals.

"Not the people who know us," Amelia said. "But sometimes we have substitute teachers."

"I don't think we need to buy you unnecessary glasses to help the occasional substitute teacher." He couldn't for the life of him figure out why someone with perfect vision would want the inconvenience of glasses.

"You could get sunglasses," Sophie said. "Daddy would let you get sunglasses."

"It's December," Amelia said.

"Tonight," Sam said. "Daddy is letting you both get a Christmas tree."

He was proud of his enthusiastic tone. It almost sounded like he was looking forward to the expedition.

"We're ready," Amelia said. She hit the remote to turn off the television.

"Did you bring home a saw?" Sophie asked, ever practical.

Sam gathered the pizza box. "I have one in my truck. You both have some old mitts that can get dirty?"

"We'll find some," Amelia called over her shoulder as

they headed through the kitchen.

Sam disposed of the carton and put the leftovers in the fridge. The girls were waiting, dressed to go, when he entered the laundry room.

He found a pair of worn leather work gloves in the bin beside the door. "Are you ready to go?"

"Yes!" They scrambled through the door and down the short staircase.

It was a fifteen-minute drive to the edge of town and the Harry farm. The forecast was for several inches of snow, and it was already falling hard, building up on the streets and sidewalks. He had a snowplow blade in the garage, and he was thinking it might be time to put it on the truck.

Pulling up, he could see they weren't the only ones who had decided to buy a tree tonight. He steeled himself at the sight of so many other cars. Some of them he recognized, the Atkinsons' and the Darrows' among others. He expected they'd want to talk to him, feel him out, gauge how he was doing as the holiday season grew close.

He knew everybody meant well. They were good people, and they were anxious to see him to move on with his life. They had the best of intentions, but he wasn't nearly ready to move on. He'd loved Kara with all his heart, and it was his fault she'd died. How was a man supposed to move on from that?

He'd barely shut off the engine and his daughters were bouncing out of the truck.

"Let's take the snowman path," Amelia shouted out.

"Come on, Daddy. Come on," Sophie called over her shoulder.

Sam wasn't worried about losing them. The area was fenced, and the paths were well lit. The Christmas tree forest was filled with friends and neighbors. The girls would know nearly everyone here.

"Sam?" came a familiar voice from behind him.

Sam tensed, mentally preparing himself for the first of what was sure to be several uncomfortable conversations tonight. He neutralized his features before turning.

"It's great to see you." His friend Brock Montrose grasped his hand.

Brock's wife Melanie came forward as well, a bright smile on her face. She was dressed in a bright purple ski jacket with a white knit hat. "Hi, Sam."

Sam gave her a quick hug.

"How've you been?" she asked, drawing back. "The girls are here with you?"

"They just took off down the path," Sam said. "Libby?" he asked, noting their six and four year old sons by their side, but not seeing their daughter.

"She's off inspecting the trees," Melanie said with a laugh. "How *are* you?"

"I'm fine," he answered heartily, giving her a broad smile. "We're picking the tree."

"Aren't we all?" She watched him closely.

He loved Melanie and Brock, but he hated being the object of pity.

"Daddy, Daddy," came Amelia's high voice.

Sam turned, grateful for the distraction.

"We found Libby," Amelia said. "They're getting a tree tonight, too."

"Hello, Libby," Sam said. Then he looked to the boys. "And hello to Grant and Foster. How are you boys?"

"I'm fine," six-year-old Grant answered dutifully.

Foster plunked his thumb into his mouth and clung silently to his mother's leg.

Sam didn't blame him. Grant had barely turned four when Sam and the girls moved out of the house next door to the Montrose's. Foster wouldn't even remember them.

"Can we have some hot chocolate?" Sophie asked.

"They have marshmallows," Libby sang out.

"Sure you can," Sam said.

"Me too, Mommy," Grant said.

Melanie gave Sam a helpless grin. "All part of the experience."

"All part," he agreed.

The three girls scampered away. Melanie followed with the two boys.

"So, what's up?" Brock sounded serious, getting down to it, the way Brock always did. It was why Sam tried to avoid him.

"It's all good," Sam said, making a show of watching the

girls talking and laughing as they joined the hot chocolate lineup.

"What do you mean good? You haven't been near your place in weeks, probably more like months."

"I've been busy," Sam answered casually. "The shop's slammed with orders."

"Libby misses the twins."

A wave of guilt hit Sam. The three girls had been insepa-rable since they'd learned to walk. Brock and Melanie had been his and Kara's best friends. They'd spent countess days in each other's backyards, countless evenings sprawled in one of their living rooms, watching movies on sleepovers. They'd shared picnics on the beach and drives to the aquarium. Seeing each other at school and on occasion, wasn't the same thing.

"I'm—" Sam started, but he couldn't finish.

Brock clamped an understanding hand on Sam's shoul-der. "Toughing it out on your own isn't going to make it any easier.

Sam pulled a breath into his tight chest. "Nothing will make it easier."

"I wish you'd let us help. Or at least let me help. I get that you can't come back to the house right now."

"I'm too busy to—"

"You're not too busy for lunch. Everybody's got to eat. Or a beer. We can meet for a beer anytime you want."

Brock wasn't helping. He was making Sam feel even

worse. It was bad enough that he missed Kara so much that his bones ached, bad enough that Christmas was almost upon them and he could barely be a decent father, but now he had to feel guilty for blowing off his best friend.

"Is there any way to make it worse?" Brock asked in an undertone.

Sam hoped not. He didn't think he could tolerate feeling any worse.

"I'm guessing the answer is no," Brock continued. "So why not give it a shot? Have a beer with me. We talk about anything or nothing. But you've got to try something, man. Anything's better than gritting your teeth through the next ten days." He paused. "Your kids deserve better than that."

That criticism hit Sam harder than anything could. He knew Brock was counting on that as a way to shake him up. But he also knew Brock was right. Amelia and Sophie deserved better than Sam had been giving.

He knew a beer wouldn't help. But Brock was a loyal friend who was trying hard to help. The least Sam could do was meet him half way.

"Okay," he agreed. "Let's have a beer."

"Tomorrow," Brock said.

"Tomorrow," Sam agreed, knowing it was better to get it over with.

JASMINE HAD FOUND a pathway off the tarmac that wound

its way through the quiet woods. Snow clung to the delicate tree branches surrounding her, shining against hundreds of tiny white lights that decorated the edges of the pathway. The flakes were falling harder now, growing in size, giving a fairyland sparkle to the scene.

Around a corner, a colorful gazebo appeared. It was decked out for the season and unbelievably beautiful. She picked up her pace and walked into the magical scene. Surrounded by color and light, she tipped her head back, holding out her tongue to catch a snowflake. Wind whispered, muted through the trees, and a feeling of calm enveloped her.

She opened her eyes again and stared at it all for a long time. Then as the cold seeped in, she made her way past ice sculptures, snowmen, and a whimsical miniature train.

Beyond the clearing, the woods opened up. A wider pathway led to the airport parking lot that wrapped around the small terminal building. The parked cars were covered in a thick layer of snow. The owners must have been gone for a while. She imagined them as passengers on an outbound flight, maybe to Florida or the Caribbean.

She felt a brief flash of envy. She'd never spent Christmas on a beach. There were far too many holiday duties for the royal family in Vollan.

The thought drew her back into her real life. The king's children's gala would be next weekend, and she'd spend two days at those events. She was happiest talking one-on-one to the children, seeing the excitement shining in their eyes, hearing their hopes and dreams for Christmas morning.

She would also attend the capital city's symphony and choir night, ride in the parade, and sit with her father, her uncle, and her cousin Adara during Christmas Eve services. The list went on and on.

She savored the last few moments of peace, knowing the interlude was over, and she had to head back to the plane. Hopefully, she'd be able to sleep most of the way to Vollan. It would help to be sharp when she got home. Her father would have questions. He'd expect an explanation.

She hoped she could come up with one that made sense. Right now, all she knew was that her panic was irrational. And irrational emotions were unfathomable to the king.

From the airport parking lot, she could see the main entrance to the terminal. It seemed easier to go through the building than to retrace her steps, so she trudged along the sidewalk, snowflakes building up on her jacket, the oversized rubber boots slipping against her feet. The wind was picking up, blowing snow across her bare knees—the idea of getting inside looked better and better.

Through the glass front doors, the terminal was quiet. Two luggage carousals were still. A long bank of check-in counters stood empty. And a lone security guard was stationed at the far end of the terminal. The arrivals and departures boards showed only two flights, both were flagged as cancelled.

"Can I help you, dear?" A sixty-ish woman approached Jasmine. She wore a bright blue plaid vest over a white blouse. Her name tag identified her as "Belle" in stylized script above the words "Welcome to Tucker".

"Yes. Thank you," Jasmine answered, looking along the back wall for a likely exit. "I need to get back outside."

The woman seemed puzzled, glancing behind Jasmine to the main doors.

"Oh, not to the parking lot," Jasmine explained. "My plane is on the tarmac. I need to get back on board."

"I'm afraid all the flights are cancelled tonight," Belle said.

"Not mine. I'm traveling on a private plane."

Belle seemed to take in Jasmine's clothing. Her expression wasn't judgmental, more curious.

Jasmine was reminded of her outlandish outfit.

She smiled, feeling self-conscious as she gestured to the oversized coat and boots. "I stepped out for a breath of fresh air."

She noted the security guard was approaching them.

"Is everything okay, Belle?" the man asked as he grew close.

"This young lady says she's here to catch a plane," said Belle.

There was an odd inflection in her tone, a gentleness, as if she was taking about a child, and Jasmine realized Belle might be wondering about her mental state.

"I'm so sorry for the confusion," she told the security guard. "I'm Jasmine Arcelus. I flew in on a private plane about an hour ago. It's a diplomatic aircraft from Vollan. We're on our way home from New York, and we had to stop for a mechanical repair. Maybe you could radio the captain?"

The two exchanged a look, and Jasmine realized they weren't yet sure what to make of her. She wasn't worried. As soon as they spoke to the flight crew, everything would be cleared up.

"I can go make a call," the security guard said.

"Thank you, Nolan," Belle said. To Jasmine, she said. "Why don't we sit down?" Her voice still seemed too carefully kind.

"I haven't lost my mind," said Jasmine.

"Of course you haven't. But let's let Nolan look into it for us?"

"If you check out the window." Jasmine glanced around the terminal, looking for a place that would give a view of the tarmac. "You'll see the plane. Maybe Nolan could take me out there and confirm my story with the crew."

There had to be a simple way to work this out.

"He's coming back now," Belle said.

"There was definitely a plane that landed from Vollan," he said.

Jasmine felt a rush of relief.

"But they took off again half an hour ago," he said.

Jasmine was sure she couldn't have heard right. "They

wouldn't take off without me."

"They did, ma'am."

She staggered a step. It was more the awkward boots than anything else. But Belle reached out to steady her. The woman's hand was strangely comforting.

Had nobody checked to make sure she was on board? Did Darren think she was resting in the bedroom? She'd been told they'd have two hours on the ground.

"They have to come back," She said to Belle and Nolan. "Call them. They'll come back for me, I'm—"

"They've already left the airport's control area," Nolan said.

"Surely somebody can contact them."

"We can get a message through air traffic control," Nolan said. "But it won't help."

"They will come back for me," Jasmine assured the two.

"They can't," said Nolan. "The runway's closed. There's a blizzard coming in fast, and it's likely to shut down most of the state."

Jasmine couldn't wrap her head around his words.

Her plane was gone. They'd left her behind, and they couldn't come back.

"Don't you worry, dear," said Belle. "It'll only be a couple of days."

Disbelief took the strength from Jasmine's voice. "A couple of…days?"

"Is there someone you can call?" asked Nolan. "We can

help you find a hotel."

It hit Jasmine then that she didn't have her phone. She didn't have anything. Darren had her passport somewhere on board. She didn't carry money, didn't have credit cards. And without her phone's contact list, she didn't know anyone's number.

"She doesn't need a hotel," Belle said staunchly. "She can stay with me."

"Belle, you can't—" Nolan began.

"Nonsense," Belle said. "I most certainly can." To Jasmine, she said. "I have plenty of room. So there's no problem at all."

"I don't have any money," Jasmine felt compelled to tell the kind woman.

The royal family would, of course, pay for everything once her plane could return. But for the moment, she was destitute.

"You don't need money," Belle said. "This is an emergency."

"Can someone at least radio the plane?" she asked Nolan. "And tell them I'm here? When they find me gone, they'll be worried."

She tried not to imagine the reaction of the security detail and then her father. One simply didn't misplace the Crown Princess. Nothing remotely like this had ever happened.

"It might take a while to get through," Nolan said. "But

yes, we should be able to get them a message."

"Thank you." She was immensely grateful. "Please be sure to tell them I got off for some air. It's important that they understand. Tell them I'm safe, and please warn them about the weather."

"Oh, they'll know about the weather," said Nolan with a wry chuckle. Then he seemed to take in Jasmine's stricken expression. He sobered. "But don't worry. I'll pass on the message."

"Thank you," she said again. She turned to Belle. "And thank *you* for rescuing me."

"It's my pleasure." Belle took her hand and gave it a reassuring squeeze. "You can meet my son-in-law and my granddaughters. You'll love them."

Chapter Two

S AM PAUSED IN the laundry room that was positioned between the garage and the kitchen. He stripped off his shirt and tossed it in the laundry basket. The scent of balsam pine had permeated the fabric, reminding him of Kara and the last Christmas season they'd spent together.

His daughters had skipped inside ahead of him, their voices growing animated as they began recounting their tree cutting adventure. Clearly, Belle was home now to provide an audience.

"Daddy caught it before it hit the ground," Amelia said.

"He swore," Sophie said, excitement clear in her tone.

"I did not swear," Sam said as he entered the kitchen.

He stopped short. He'd assumed the girls were talking to Belle. Instead, he found them in conversation with an attractive, blonde stranger.

The woman was slim and maybe five-feet-four. She had full red lips, deep green eyes, and porcelain skin that looked too perfect to be real. On top of her beauty, she exuded wealth and class. Her outfit was polished to a fine sheen—a crisp white blouse, fitted blazer, and a slim skirt.

"Girls?" he asked, wondering who this woman could be, and finding himself irritated that she'd invaded the intimacy of their kitchen. It was hard enough for him to keep it together for his daughters tonight, never mind for a total stranger.

The woman glanced at his bare chest, and the faintest blush appeared in her cheeks.

"You said dang it," Amelia said.

"Dang it isn't a swear word," he told her, still cataloguing the woman.

She had bare feet. What was she doing with bare feet on a night like this?

Before he could guard against it, his hormones surged. The unfamiliar feeling rocked him to his toes. What was wrong with him? It was ridiculous to think a lavender pedicure was off the charts sexy.

"It's a cover swear," Sophie said. "We all know you meant—"

"Sophie!" Sam admonished, appalled that she might blurt out an actual swear word.

He couldn't help but glance at the woman to gauge her reaction to the conversation. She looked slightly amused, and slightly...something else. He couldn't put his finger on it, but he didn't like it. Tolerant, maybe? But who was she to tolerate them? Who *was* she?

"It's *ten feet tall*," Amelia sang out. "The *biggest* one there."

Belle came in from the living room then. She looked particularly pleased with herself, and seemed very happy to have him home. "Sam. There you are. We have company tonight."

"So I see." He failed to keep the edge from in his tone.

Belle ignored it, but it was clear the stranger had noticed.

"This is Jasmine Arcelus," said Belle. "She's been stranded in Tucker by the blizzard. The airport's closed, and the phones are down already."

His glance went briefly to the window, reconfirming the heavy snowfall. He'd heard the weather report on the drive back from the Christmas tree forest, and he knew there was a monster storm bearing down on the state.

"This is Sam," Belle said to Jasmine. "Sophie and Amelia's father."

"Hello, Sam." Jasmine's accent was soft and cultured, but he couldn't quite place it.

She held out a slim hand. He didn't want to touch her, but there was no way to avoid it. Her hand was cool, smooth, and delicate, in stark contrast to his, which was broad and scarred, and currently streaked with dirt and sap from cutting the tree.

Embarrassed, he quickly pulled away. "I'm sorry."

She looked puzzled.

"My hand is dirty." He rubbed his palm against his jeans.

She didn't check to see if he'd left a smudge on her hand. Instead, she smiled. "It's nice to meet you, Sam."

When she said his name, something pressed heavily against his chest. She was a random stranger, he told himself. He has no business having an emotional reaction to her.

"The tree is drying in the garage," Amelia said.

"It was all covered in snow," Sophie said.

"Did something happen to your shirt?" Belle asked him.

"The tree," Sam answered, suddenly acutely aware of his bare chest. "It got dirty."

He felt self-conscious standing here half-naked. Jasmine's bare feet and his bare chest made the situation feel intimate—which was absurd. There were five of them in the kitchen, and it was perfectly acceptable for a man to be shirtless in his own home. There was nothing remotely intimate about it.

"Jasmine was stranded at the airport," Belle continued. "Her plane left without her."

"Were you late?" Sophie asked Jasmine. "Daddy was late once, and he got stuck in Chicago for three days."

It surprised Sam that Sophie remembered that incident. She couldn't have been more than four at the time.

"They thought I was still on board," Jasmine said to Sophie.

"It was a private plane," Belle said.

Sam's initial guess had obviously been right. Jasmine was wealthy. Not that it explained what she was doing in the kitchen or how soon she was leaving. He wanted to be alone right now. He'd planned to put the girls to bed as soon as possible, scrub off the balsam smell in a long, hot shower, and shut himself away in his own misery.

"They had to close the airport," Jasmine said. "And your grandma was nice enough to invite me to stay."

Stay? The weight on Sam's chest grew heavier. The very last thing he wanted was an overnight guest in the house. Not tonight, and certainly not through the duration of the blizzard.

"You're pretty," Sophie said.

Jasmine gave a gracious smile at the compliment. "Thank you. You're very pretty, too."

"Daddy says being pretty's not important," Amelia said.

Sam was embarrassed by Amelia's bluntness. "That's not exactly what I said."

"Yes, you did," Sophie said. She tapped her index finger against her temple, an almost comically sage expression coming over her young face. "You said being pretty's not important. It's what's up here that counts."

"I was making a point about doing your arithmetic homework."

He didn't want to have this conversation. He wanted to be alone. He needed some sleep. Then tomorrow he'd fight once again to make it through the season. He wished he'd never agreed to that beer with Brock. All he wanted was to be left alone.

"Have you done your homework?" Belle asked the girls.

Sam knew it wasn't a rebuke of his parenting, but it felt

like one.

"We only just got back," said Sophie.

"Then this way," said Belle, hustling the girls toward the living room and the main staircase to their bedroom.

Sam was suddenly left alone with Jasmine.

Great. Was he her official host now?

Neither of them spoke for a moment.

"It was very generous of Belle to invite me to stay," Jasmine said.

"She's generous to a fault." The words sounded rude even to Sam, but he didn't seem to be able to muster up false hospitality.

"I hope it won't be for long."

Once again, Sam found himself glancing out the window, gauging the snowfall. "They may declare a state of emergency."

"Is that bad?"

He looked back at her in disbelief. "It's an *emergency*."

"You don't need to be sarcastic."

"How could it be anything but bad?" He didn't know what was wrong with him. His mouth seemed to be running amuck.

She didn't answer. But hurt flitted through her eyes. She took a step backward. "Maybe you could just tell me—" She stopped, obviously at a loss.

"I'll show you the guest room."

"I don't want to be any trouble. Belle made it sound like

you had plenty of room."

"We do." He made to pass her, but she moved at the same time, and they collided.

She stumbled and gave a little gasp.

He automatically reached to steady her, grasping her arm. Their gazes met, and a surge of sensual awareness passed through him.

He instantly let her go, stepping back.

"My fault," she said. A flush came over her face.

"I was going to lead the way," he said.

She stepped to one side. "Please do."

"It's through the living room. Just give me a second." He rounded the island counter, backtracking to the laundry room to pull a faded t-shirt over his head. He felt a little more in control being fully dressed.

He led her through the large, high-ceilinged living room. They took the short hallway that passed the dining room to the guest room which was across from Belle's master suite.

He opened the door to a white, airy room with rich carpeting, a canopied bed, two cream colored armchairs, and a private bathroom.

"This is much nicer than I expected," she said, gazing around as she walked in.

"You thought we were impoverished?"

She didn't react to his challenge, but kept walking toward the big windows. "It's more than I need."

"But not more than you deserve?"

She turned. "Have I done something to offend you?"

Though her question was blunt, she delivered it was poise and grace.

Other than invading his space while he was in a particularly foul mood, truth was, she hadn't.

"I've had a long day," he said. He knew she deserved an apology, and he searched for the appropriate words.

"I understand," she said. "Please don't let me keep you from whatever it is you need to do."

He knew Belle would never forgive him for abandoning her. "Have you eaten?"

"Please don't worry about me. You've done enough already."

"I'll take that as a no."

She didn't answer.

"When did you last eat anything?" He persisted.

"New York City."

That didn't give him a timeframe, but he guessed it had been a while ago.

"We have leftover pizza," he offered.

She looked intrigued by the simple statement. In fact, she smiled.

He wished she wouldn't do that. He liked her smile, and he was trying to stay annoyed with her. He didn't want anyone new inside his world this week, least of all a pretty woman who had somehow managed to remind him he was a man.

"I've never had that," she said.

"You've never had pizza?"

"I've never had leftover pizza. Is it from a restaurant?"

"Luigi's over on Main Street."

"Do you eat it cold?" she asked.

"Are you messing with me?"

"What do you mean?"

"I mean, you're acting like takeout pizza is some exotic dish. Are you a Quaker or something?" As he asked the question, he couldn't imagine Quakers would get lavender pedicures.

"I'm a Presbyterian. I'd love to try cold pizza." She looked like she would.

For some reason, a bit of tension eased from him. "Then follow me." He gestured with his arm to usher her back to the kitchen.

They'd ordered ham and pineapple. It was Amelia's favorite, and it had been her turn to choose. Sam put a slice on a plate at the breakfast bar for Jasmine then decided on one for himself as well.

"Beer?" he asked, as she lifted herself onto the high chair.

"If that's the correct pairing."

He couldn't tell if she was being deliberately snooty or not. "It's what I'm drinking."

"Then I'll take it," she said agreeably.

He was starting to wonder what to make of her.

He opened two bottles of lager and set them out with the

pizza. He left the rest of the pizza on the counter in case she wanted more.

He sat down, and she glanced around the breakfast bar.

"Is it really eaten with your hands?"

"You are messing with me, aren't you?"

"Why would I be messing with you? I'm a guest in your house, and I don't want to be rude."

"As in New York," he said, "using a knife and fork would be rude."

"Okay." She squared herself up to the plate, sizing it up, looking as if she was going to duel with the slice of pizza rather than eat it.

She glanced at him.

He rolled his eyes and lifted his slice, bending it slightly in half. "Like this."

"That looks easy."

"I'm sure you'll do fine."

She emulated his hold and took a bite of the pizza.

She swallowed and smiled. "That is good." Then she took a sip of the beer.

"Well?" he asked.

"It pairs nicely."

"I'm so relieved." He didn't want to engage in small talk, and he sure didn't want to get to know her, but he couldn't stop himself from asking. "Where are you from?"

JASMINE WASN'T SURE how much to reveal about her identity. It was obvious Sam didn't want her in his home, equally obvious she was annoying him. She didn't think he was genuinely interested in her answer.

There were also security considerations. She was completely on her own here in Tucker. She'd never been anywhere without security. And she always had Darren or another aide close by. It was strange to be alone. She had no idea what would happen if people learned she was royalty.

She decided it was safest to keep her answers vague. "I'm from Vollan."

"Where is that? I can't place your accent."

"Vollan is a small country in northern Europe." She took another bite of the pizza, realizing how hungry she'd become.

"Were you born there?"

"I was."

"You must be rich or important or both."

Jasmine gave a small shrug to dismiss the notion. "My father is quite well known."

"So it's family money?"

She chose her words carefully. "We have land mostly. It's been passed down through a lot of generations. What about you?"

He stretched out one of his hands as if it was part of the answer to her question. "I'm a carpenter."

His hand looked strong and capable, a little battered

perhaps, but there was something reassuring about its strength.

"You build things."

There was a note of defensiveness in his tone. "I get my hands dirty, if that's what you're asking."

"It wasn't." She took another bite, letting her annoyance dissipate.

It was a trick she'd learned at a very young age. When a conversation became delicate, slow things down. Never get upset, and never let your emotions show.

He took a swallow of his beer, plunking the bottle down on the countertop. His tone was sharp. "I'm guessing we're not the kind of people you're used to."

She waited another beat, taking a breath, lowering her shoulders and relaxing her core. What he said wasn't true. She interacted with people from all walks of life.

"Why would you guess that?" she asked him.

"You look…" He seemed to search for the right words. "Expensive."

She couldn't help but smile at the pained expression on his face. "Did you mean that as an insult?"

"I meant it as an observation."

"Well…" She took a moment to size him up. "You look functional. And I mean that as a compliment."

"How magnanimous of you."

"You are determined to fight with me, aren't you?"

People were never so brazen with her. She should probably have been insulted, but she was intrigued instead.

"I'll be honest with you," Sam said.

"You may do that."

He drew back. "Did you just grant me permission?"

She realized she had. "Go on."

"I want to be left alone tonight. I really don't want company. I certainly wasn't expecting a houseguest, and having you here looking down your nose at me with Christmas around the corner is the last thing I need in my life." His voice rose combatively on the last few words.

Jasmine struggled to cover her astonishment at his tone.

"Sam!" Belle's voice interrupted them from the doorway. "What has gotten into you?"

Sam came to his feet, regret clear on his face as he spoke to Jasmine. "My apologies."

"No, no." Jasmine waved his words away. She was the one who had invaded his privacy, and it was obviously a big inconvenience. "I'm the one who should apologize for intruding."

He drained his beer glass and took his empty plate to the sink.

"Jasmine," Belle said, moving closer. "You are welcome in our home for as long as you'd like. Don't let Sam's bad mood upset you."

Sam stood facing the sink. He was gripping the lip of the counter, tension straining his shoulders against the thin t-shirt.

Though it was obvious his distress went beyond their conversation, Jasmine regretted her part in upsetting him.

He turned abruptly.

"Goodnight," he said, gaze straight ahead as he marched from the room.

"I don't know what happened," Jasmine said to Belle after Sam had left.

Belle gave her a comforting squeeze on the shoulder as she took the chair next to her. "It's not your fault. The holidays are a difficult time for him."

"He misses his wife?" Jasmine guessed.

Nobody had said a word about the girls' mother. And since they were living in Sam's mother-in-law's house, a divorce seemed unlikely. That left a sad possibility.

"We lost her two years ago," Belle said.

"I'm so sorry to hear that."

Jasmine would have liked to ask what happened, but she didn't want to pry. She'd lost her own mother when she was only six, and her heart went out to Sophie and Amelia.

"I'm not making an excuse for him," Belle said. "But I am giving you the reason. The closer Christmas comes, the more upset he gets. He's trying to hide it from the girls, but they can see it happening."

"Perhaps I should find somewhere else to stay," Jasmine said.

The last thing she wanted to do was to make the family's life more difficult. It was the middle of the night in Vollan, and there was no phone service in Tucker. But she'd try to get through to the palace first thing in the morning. Perhaps they could wire funds. Then she could move to a hotel and leave Sam and his family in peace.

"Nonsense," Belle said. "Life has to go on. I'm coming to the conclusion Sam's been coddled long enough. It's time for some tough love."

Jasmine wasn't comfortable getting anywhere near Belle's intervention into Sam's life. He was a grown man and he should be able to decide the pace of his own recovery. She couldn't imagine the pain of losing the love of your life. She knew her own father had never fully recovered from losing Queen Katerina.

"Grandma?"

One of the twins appeared in the kitchen. Jasmine couldn't tell if it was Sophie or Amelia. She'd identified them by their clothes earlier, but this little girl was wearing a set of pale blue pajamas with red piping.

"You should be asleep, sweetheart," Belle said. But even as she spoke she held her arms out to her granddaughter.

The little girl climbed into Belle's lap.

"Amelia?" Jasmine guessed.

"You got it right." Amelia smiled.

Belle kissed the top of her head. "Is something wrong?"

"Can we go to our old house tomorrow? I know Daddy won't like it, but maybe we don't have to tell him."

Jasmine expected Belle to caution Amelia against keeping

secrets from her father. Surprisingly, she didn't.

"Why do you want to go to the house?" Belle asked.

"The Christmas ornaments," Amelia said. "I asked Daddy if we could get them. But his face went all funny, and he didn't answer. Sophie wants the ones she made that time, the little elves and the bells." She took a breath. "And the one with Mommy's picture on it."

Jasmine's chest contracted at the little girl's words, squeezing around her heart.

"I remember them," Belle said, stroking Amelia's hair.

"Sophie's sad," said Amelia. "And Daddy's sad. But it could make Daddy happy. Don't you think maybe? It could make Daddy happy to remember Mommy. He says he loved Mommy."

"He did love your mommy."

Amelia tipped her head to look up at Belle. "Can we go get them?"

Belle's gaze met Jasmine's.

Jasmine wished she had something wise to say. She didn't.

"Let me think about how we might do that," Belle said.

Amelia gave a hesitant smile. "I think we can make it a fun Christmas."

"I think we can, too," Belle said.

Amelia slipped from her lap and padded from the kitchen.

After a moment, Belle spoke to Jasmine. "It's complicated."

"You don't have to explain anything to me."

Jasmine realized the best thing for her to do was leave as soon as she could in the morning. This family had enough to deal with without her complicating things. She stepped down from the high seat and, as Sam had done, she took her plate and glass to the kitchen sink.

"You'll need something to sleep in," Belle said, coming briskly to her feet. "There's a new toothbrush in the guest bathroom, plenty of fresh towels, and I put a clean nightgown on the bed. It's mine. Probably not the most stylish thing in the world, but it should keep you warm."

"You've been so kind," Jasmine said.

"Anybody would do the same thing." Belle responded. "You get a good night's sleep, and we'll see what's what in the morning. It's supposed to be the last day of school before the holidays, but I think every child in town is hoping for a snow day."

Jasmine knew it wasn't true that anybody would have done the same thing. Belle seemed like a rare person. It was pitch-dark beyond the kitchen window now, impossible to tell what the weather was doing. But given the earlier reports, it seemed likely the town's children would get their wish, meaning Jasmine might still be trapped in Tucker tomorrow.

SAM POWERED DOWN his random orbit sander and wiped

the bedside table top with a clean cloth. He set the power tool aside and pulled off his safety goggles to assess the finish and pattern of the wood.

"Were you planning to skip our lunch?" Brock's voice surprised Sam.

Sam had seriously considered doing just that, but he wasn't about to admit it. "Just finishing up."

"Then my timing is perfect." Brock paused to check out the finish on the table.

Brock was a professional firefighter, but he was also a decent carpenter. He and Sam had worked on many backyard projects together, furniture, the deck, a playhouse for the girls in the backyard. But that was before Kara had died, back when Sam could stand to look at his backyard.

"I'll wash up," Sam said.

"This is nice," Brock said. "An out of town client?"

"This one's going to Boston. They ordered a whole bedroom set."

"You really need to hire some help."

"I've been thinking about it." Sam lied. He used to have several employees, and his business had been growing, but these days he preferred to work alone.

"Am I right in guessing demand has been going up and up since the television coverage?"

"It didn't hurt," Sam answered over his shoulder as he made his way to the restroom.

A local television station had included him in a piece on

Maine small businesses. The segment on him happened to be picked up by a national network. Traffic on Sam's website had taken an immediate spike, and orders had been pouring in steadily ever since. Customers now had a year-long waiting period.

He knew an assistant would help him meet demand. But he wasn't in this for the money. He needed to make a decent living for himself and his daughters, and he could do that by himself.

"You should take on an apprentice." Brock had followed him and stood in the open door of the restroom.

"That would only slow me down." Sam lathered up his hands.

"Not if you also hired a couple more tradesmen. You're highly skilled, Sam. You should teach your techniques to others."

"Maybe." Sam twisted on the taps to rinse his hands.

"You're lying to me."

"That's because you're hassling me."

Brock held up his palms in mock surrender. "Fair enough. I'll stop."

"Good."

"I hear you have a houseguest."

Sam's thoughts jumped to Jasmine, a picture blooming in his mind before he could stop it. She'd gotten under his skin last night. So much so, he'd had a hard time falling asleep. He'd kept rehashing their conversations, alternating between feeling annoyed with her for showing up and guilty about his rude behavior.

She must have formed a low opinion of him. But that was just as well. Maybe she'd avoid him now.

"It's all over town," Brock continued, "that Belle rescued her from the airport. I hear she's a ten."

"I thought the phones were down and everybody was snowed in."

How could gossip have made its way around town so efficiently? Sam had been forced to attach his snowplow blade to the front of his pickup truck to clear his own pathway to work this morning.

"Main Street's open. At least for the time being. There's no letup in the snowfall yet, but enough people walked into town to keep things open. Christmas shopping doesn't stop for a storm."

"Are the phones still out?" Sam asked, brushing past talk of Christmas. He hadn't had a reason to check his cell this morning.

"Everything's down. We're lucky we have local power. The state grid has taken a hit. There are a whole lot of blacked out areas between here and Philadelphia."

Sam dried off his hands. "Anything open for lunch?"

Brock held up a paper bag. "I brought subs and soft drinks."

Sam was pleasantly surprised. He was happy to eat here in the shop. There were too many people he might run into in the Main Street restaurants, too many people who might stop by their table and ask how he was doing. He didn't want to make up answers to that question. All he wanted was a little space.

"So, tell me about her." Brock led the way to Sam's small, windowless office and parked himself at one of the two battered chairs set around a utilitarian table.

The two men had shared countless lunches and after work drinks here, and Sam experienced a wave of nostalgia. It had been a long time since he'd sat across a table and talked to Brock. Astonishingly, it felt pretty good.

"Her private jet took off and left her behind." Sam could hear the mocking tone in his own voice.

"So I hear. Is she some billionaire's trophy wife?"

Funny, that had never even occurred to Sam. He'd had no reason to check for a ring, but he'd assumed she was single. She certainly hadn't struck him as the type to marry for money. Maybe that was because she struck him as the type who'd had money all her life.

He took the chair across from Brock, stretching his legs beneath the table and rotating his shoulders. His muscles appreciated the break.

"Didn't sound like she married into it," he said. "She told me the money had been in the family for generations."

Brock was clearly surprised. "You asked about her money?"

"In a roundabout way."

Sam accepted a sandwich from Brock and helped himself to a cola, popping the top of the can before unwrapping the turkey bacon sub.

"What does that mean?"

"She's got a funny snobbery element to her. It's like, she knows she shouldn't be that way, and she's trying hard to mingle with the peasants, but she just can't help herself, you know?"

"So, you asked?"

"So, I asked."

Brock looked unimpressed. "Did she ask about *your* money?"

Sam took the point. The more hours that went past, the worse Sam felt about his behavior last night.

"She asked me what I did for a living," he said.

"And you told her."

"Of course I told her. I'm not ashamed of being a carpenter."

Brock looked genuinely astonished. "Why would you be?"

"It felt a little funny last night. She had the private jet, and the perfect hair, makeup, what were obviously very expensive clothes. And no shoes. Does that seem weird to you? She had bare feet, with these pretty purple toenails. The whole outfit was beyond perfect, but what the heck happened to her shoes?"

Brock gazed at him for a moment with an expression of

puzzlement. "Did you ask?"

"No, I didn't. It seemed, I don't know, too intimate a question."

"But you did ask her about her money?"

"She said her father was well-known in her country, so I asked her if it was family money. She said it was in land, passed down through a bunch of generations."

"And you didn't think that was too intimate?" Brock asked.

"It didn't seem like it at the time," Sam said. Though, in retrospect, it had certainly been brash. He wasn't usually one to pry into people's personal lives.

"What country?" Brock asked. "Where's she from?"

"Somewhere called Vollan in northern Europe."

"I'll have to brush up on my geography."

"I guess."

Sam bit into his sandwich. The bun was fresh, the veggies crisp, and the bacon blended with the mayo to give a satisfying smoky flavor.

"How are the girls?" Brock asked.

"Good. They're good. Belle likes having them with her." Sam knew he was defending his living arrangements, but he couldn't seem to help himself.

"Libby keeps asking when you're coming back."

"I have to finish the renovations." Sam's stomach clenched down, and the sandwich didn't seem so appetizing anymore.

"Need a hand?" Brock asked with studied casualness.

"I'm fine."

"Sam."

"Don't."

"You can't put it off forever."

"I'm *not* putting it off."

Brock dropped his sandwich onto the wrapper, frowning as he rocked back in his chair. "You want me to do it? I can replace the wall for you."

"No!" Sam all but shouted. He set down his own sandwich. "This was a bad idea."

"No, it wasn't. Talk to me, Sam."

"What is there to say?" Sam shot up from his chair, knocking it over backward with a clatter against the concrete floor. "She's dead, and I killed her."

"That's ridiculous, and you know it's ridiculous."

"I should have been driving that night. We all know I should have been driving."

"You'd had a couple of drinks. You couldn't drive."

"Then I shouldn't have been drinking. I should have taken care of my family." Sam's voice went raw.

"The trucker ran a stop sign."

Once again, Sam saw the bright lights, heard the air horn, felt the sickening thud of the impact. The world had spun in a circle, and for long minutes he didn't know if all four of them were going to be killed.

"I could have avoided it," he said bleakly. "If I'd been

driving, I could have avoided it."

"You don't know that. It's impossible for you to know that."

"But I do. I *do* know it."

Brock stood with him, coming close, clasping a hand tightly on his shoulder.

Sam fought an urge to shake him off. Brock was his best friend, and he was trying to help. He was dead wrong, but Sam knew he was trying his best.

"I know it's pointless for me to say this," Brock said. "But you've got to shake it off."

Sam stared at him. That was impossible. Brock had to know just how impossible that was.

"Let's say it was your fault," Brock said.

A huge weight suddenly lifted from Sam's shoulders. Finally, after all this time, somebody besides him had admitted it.

"Thank you." His voice came out hoarse.

Brock's hand squeezed tighter, as if he could pull Sam out of his misery.

"I don't want you to feel this way." Brock's voice was as raw as Sam's. "I hate that you feel this way. If it was Melanie. I don't know. I might feel exactly the way you do. And I might blame myself. And maybe you could have avoided it if you'd been driving. But it doesn't change anything. You have two young girls depending on you."

Sam's throat closed up at the thought of his daughters.

"You're all they've got. I'm not asking you to forget. I'm not asking you to turn on a dime. I'm asking you to take one small step. Go back to your house. Tear something down. Put something up. Do one small thing, just one small thing to get past the logjam."

Sam knew he couldn't do it. But he nodded anyway. He was willing to lie to his best friend to get out of this conversation.

Brock gave a cold chuckle. "You're the worst liar in the world."

Sam didn't have an answer for that.

"It doesn't have to be today, and it doesn't have to be tomorrow." Brock let go of Sam's shoulder and moved back to his chair at the table. "But I'm going to ask again. I'm going to ask again, because it's my duty as your friend."

"Okay." Sam could agree to that.

It wasn't anything different than he'd been telling himself for weeks now. Get back into his house and begin to repair what he'd broken.

Chapter Three

"**Y**OU COULD HELP us build a snowman," Amelia said from where she was kneeling backward on a sofa, arms propped along the back, gazing out the bay window into the front yard.

The question turned Jasmine's thoughts to what Darren or Costa Rhys, the head of her security detail, would think of her leaving the house unprotected in these circumstances. She knew they'd tell her no. They'd definitely tell her to stay put.

But neither Darren nor Costa were here right now. And there was no way to ask their permission, since the phones and Internet had been down since last night. She remained grateful that Nolan had been able to get a message to her plane through air traffic control. If he hadn't, her father and the entire royal security service would be in an uproar.

Here in Tucker, nobody knew or cared who she was. The world was white beyond the window, with thick snow-flakes falling steadily to earth, weighing down tree branches and piling up in the yard. The sun had to be up there somewhere, but she sure couldn't see it.

Here and now, she was on her own. She could romp in the snow or do anything else she wanted, and they'd never even know about it. It was quite liberating.

"Jasmine?" Sophie prompted.

Both girls had turned their heads to look at her, anticipation in their expressions.

She considered her answer. Nobody knew she was a princess. As far as anyone here was concerned, she was a perfectly ordinary person. Surely there was no more danger to her in the front yard than there was to Amelia and Sophie.

"Sure," she said. Why not? "I'd love to build a snowman."

Both girls shrieked in delight and bounced off the sofa.

As Jasmine stood, she thought of a practical problem. "I'm afraid I don't have anything suitable to wear."

"There are tons of old clothes in the basement," Amelia said, skipping across the room to take Jasmine's hand.

"We play dress up down there all the time," Sophie said.

"It's Sophie's favorite game," Amelia said, tugging Jasmine toward the hallway.

"Will there be something to fit me?" asked Jasmine. She was only five-feet-four, but the girls were less than four feet tall.

"There's all kinds of old stuff down there," Sophie said, running ahead and sliding on her sock feet on the polished wood floor. She grasped the handle on a wide, white door and pulled it open.

The girls seemed to know exactly what they were doing, so Jasmine allowed them to lead her down a wide flight of stairs. The room was big and utilitarian, bright, with white painted walls and small windows near the ceilings. The wooden rafters were exposed, and pillars supported the structure of the house.

"Over here," said Amelia.

She let go of Jasmine's hand and led the way past shelves full of books, stored furniture, and stacks of large plastic bins, flipping on light switches as she moved. They passed through a doorway to a room that was obviously a play area. It was scattered with toys, bright area rugs, mini furniture and a big plastic playhouse.

"This is our tickle trunk," said Sophie, straining to lift the lid of a massive maple wood chest.

Jasmine quickly reached out to help, leaning the heavy lid against the wall behind it.

The girls dug through the pile of clothes inside.

"Do you play here often?" Jasmine asked, taking in all the possibilities of the big room. She could imagine dozens of games and adventures children could have in all this space. If today's weather was any indication of normal during the winter, it was wise to have an indoor play space for children.

"More when we were little," Amelia said without looking up. "Now we usually go to our friends' houses."

"You have a lot of friends?"

Sophie nodded, helping to search through the clothing.

"But they live farther away from Grandma's, so we have to drive."

"Libby used to be right next door."

"Libby is one of your friends?" Jasmine asked.

"Our best friend," said Amelia. "But then Mommy…"

The girls glanced at each other.

Jasmine crouched down between them. "I was very sorry to hear that your Mommy died."

"She was pretty," Sophie said in a soft voice.

"She's in heaven now," Amelia said.

"Yes, she is," Jasmine agreed.

"Daddy's sad," Sophie said.

"I'm very sorry to hear that, too."

Jasmine's thoughts moved to Sam and the wall he'd immediately thrown up when they met. It was obvious he was hurt and angry, and she was clearly an unwanted and very temporary presence in his life. Still, even knowing that, there was something about him that called to her, something that made her want to know him and help him. It didn't make sense, but the urge was strong all the same.

When they'd accidentally collided yesterday in the kitchen, she'd felt a surge of heat, a sexual awareness she'd never experienced before. It could have been because Sam was a fit, attractive man. By any definition, he was a sexy man. Then again, maybe it had nothing to do with Sam himself.

The men in her country would never touch her that way. They'd never accidentally bump into her. They respected a significant perimeter around any member of the royal family.

"These are really big," Amelia said, drawing out a pair of black and white checkerboard slacks and holding them up. "They might fit you."

Jasmine banished the memories of Sam's touch, focusing instead on the girls and their planned snow adventure. The slacks did look as if they might fit.

"This would be warm," Sophie said. She'd found a roomy black sweatshirt with a faded gold sports logo on the front.

"It looks rather big," Jasmine said, thinking she'd swim in it.

"But it's warm," Amelia said. "And it's cold outside."

Jasmine supposed she didn't need to be fashionable to build a snowman. As she contemplated the sweat shirt, her attention was caught by a flash of color in a corner of the room. She saw it was a rack of extravagant dresses, pinks and mauves, along with black and white, next to jewel tones of blue and green. She moved to get a better look at them.

"Are those some of your dress-up clothes?"

"They're mostly from when Grandma was a girl," Amelia said.

"Belle wore these?" Jasmine was surprised. Belle had struck her as a very practical woman. "They're very beautiful."

"She was a dancer," Sophie said. "We're allowed to wear them now."

"Sophie really likes them," Amelia said.

"You don't like them?" Jasmine couldn't imagine how any little girl wouldn't fall in love with such a fun array of costumes.

"They're not very practical," Amelia said with a sniff.

"They're not supposed to be practical," Sophie said.

Jasmine lifted one of the hangers, examining a deep green dress. The full, tulle skirt sparkled with sequins. The top was satin, with a scooped neckline, held up by cap sleeves.

"That one's too big for us," Sophie said. "But this is my favorite." She showed Jasmine an aqua gown with a full, flowing skirt, a floral top, and short, bubble sleeves.

"Will you try it on for me?" Jasmine asked, seeing Sophie's enthusiasm.

"I like this one," Amelia said, choosing a navy blue gown with crisscrossed silver beading. Dress-up might not be her favorite game, but it was clear she didn't want to be left out.

"I'd love to see it on you," Jasmine told her.

While the girls scrambled into the dresses, Jasmine noticed a small, pink makeup table with a mirror, hair accessories, and a few cosmetics.

"I could style your hair." She offered to Sophie, who was first into her dress.

Sophie scampered over and turned her back to Jasmine. "Zip me up."

Jasmine pulled up the zipper of the dress, straightening

the sleeves and smoothing out the skirt.

"You look very pretty," she told Sophie.

"Can you do me a braid?" asked Sophie, her excitement obviously mounting.

"Yes, I can."

Jasmine sat down on a little stood and beckoned Sophie closer while she located a hairbrush.

"Will you put it on top of my head?" asked Sophie, lifting a big handful of her blond hair. "I like it on top of my head."

"Let's see what we can do." Jasmine took stock of the supplies and made a plan for a simple hairstyle.

"I want my braid to dangle down my back," Amelia said.

She also presented her back to Jasmine and Jasmine zipped up her dress.

It took most of an hour, but Jasmine got each of the girls dressed up. She even added a little lipstick to their mouths and some blue shadow to their eyes. They jockeyed for position in front of the mirror, chirping with delight at what they saw.

"Now you," Sophie said.

Jasmine laughed. "I don't need to dress up."

"You should be get pretty, too." Amelia considered the rack and then chose a deep purple gown. "This one. Mommy used to wear it when she played with us."

In an instant, Jasmine realized what she'd done. The girls had probably played dress-up here for years. They must have played it with their mother while she was alive. Jasmine could have easily upset them with painful memories. She could still upset them.

She pasted a bright smile on her face. "I thought we were going to build a snowman?" She quickly located the checkerboard pants and pulled off the suede slippers Belle had lent her. She stepped into the pants and drew them up beneath her skirt.

"They fit," she told the girls, hoping to distract them. She unzipped her skirt and pulling it down to get out of it.

"Snowman time." Amelia sang out.

Sophie looked decidedly disappointed. "I want to make tea."

"It's going to get dark soon," Amelia said.

"We could make tea after we build the snowman." Jasmine offered.

Trying to keep the momentum going, she pulled on the sweatshirt. It was worn, supple, and it smelled earthy and pleasant.

She did a pirouette. "How do I look?"

"Cute," Sophie said.

"Funky," Amelia added.

"I don't know that I've ever looked funky before."

Jasmine rather liked the description.

"Let's go." Amelia reached for her zipper to get out of the dress.

Without giving them a chance to hesitate, Jasmine

quickly unzipped both girls. "Let's build a giant snowman before it gets dark."

"We'll surprise Daddy," Amelia said.

Sophie sighed in what looked like resignation, while Jasmine felt like she'd dodged a bullet. She was going to have to be careful around these two. The last thing she wanted was to inadvertently bring back memories that could hurt them.

IT WAS DARK when Sam arrived home, but the front of the house was lit up, and through the haze of falling snow he could make out three figures dashing across the front yard. The girls were playing and the sight made him smile. It was reassuringly ordinary at the end of a difficult day.

In the glow of the bay window, he could see the outline of a big snowman. They'd obviously been busy for a while now.

He parked his truck and came around the side of the house to join them.

He caught only the briefest glimpse of Amelia before he was hit full in the face by a snowball. Both of his daughters shrieked with laughter.

Before his vision cleared, he was reaching down to make his own snowball and join in the fight. As he stood, he caught a glimpse of ugly checkerboard pants on a pair of legs between the two girls. They were Kara's pants and his heart tripped in his chest.

"Run, Jasmine, run!" Sophie shouted.

"He'll get you," Amelia called.

Jasmine was laughing. But then his expression must have registered, and she sobered. She could obviously tell something was wrong.

He'd thought she was Kara. For a split second, he'd actually thought Kara had somehow come back to him. He realized that was crazy. He also knew it wasn't healthy.

"Sam?" Jasmine's question was tentative as she took a small step toward him.

In a blinding flash, he acknowledged that Brock had been right.

Brock was his best friend and his hard message to Sam today was completely on target. It was time for Sam to climb out of his grief. Some way, somehow, he had to accept Kara's death and start to rebuild his life.

He was going to do it. And it was going to start right now.

"You better run." He warned Jasmine in a dire tone, lobbing a soft one her way.

She easily dodged it and tossed her own snowball back at him.

It hit him dead in the chest, splattering apart on contact. The woman had a decent arm.

He scooped up another and threw it more firmly, catching her in the stomach.

Then his daughters came at him from both sides, throwing snowballs at his head. Amelia's hit the mark, while Sophie's missed. He scooped them both around the waist and lifted them into the air.

"Who wants a face-wash?"

"Not me, not me," they both cried out, wiggling to get away.

He held them fast. "Then you shouldn't have started this fight."

"Did you see our snowman?" Sophie asked.

"Come and look at him," Amelia said.

"You're trying to distract me." He accused them.

"Jasmine helped us," Sophie said.

Sam found his gaze moving to Jasmine.

Close up, in the soft light bouncing off the snow, she was an arrestingly beautiful woman. Her cheeks were flushed, her lips dark red, and her eyes glowed a crystalline shade of green. Her blond hair was covered in a red knit hat, but wisps had escaped and swirled around her face.

Her gaze was slightly wary as it met his, and he had the unsettling feeling that she could see through his act.

Whether she could or not was irrelevant, he assured himself. She wasn't likely to call him on it, and neither would anyone else. He was moving forward. He was faking an emotional recovery until it became true. Using whatever emotional strength he could muster, he was working towards accepting the reality of his world and becoming the father his girls deserved.

"Show me the snowman." He set both of his daughters down on the ground, using the excuse to break his gaze from Jasmine.

The girls trotted awkwardly across the yard in their snow boots and nylon pants.

"Belle says the airport's still closed," Jasmine told him, an apology in her tone.

"I heard that, too."

"And the telephones are still out. If I could have, I would have contacted my family to send me some money—"

"You don't need any money." He regretted his churlish behavior last night.

Belle had been right to call him on it. Jasmine was stranded in Tucker through no fault of her own. It didn't matter that it was inconvenient for him. Common decency demanded he offer her shelter.

"It would be better if I went to a hotel," Jasmine said.

"Can you see Belle agreeing to that?" he asked.

The question earned him a small smile. Jasmine had an extraordinarily pretty smile.

"It's taller than me," Amelia called out, holding her mitten-covered hand to her head and demonstrating the difference between her and the snowman.

"I think it's taller than me," Sam said.

"Stand beside him, Daddy," Sophie said.

Sam moved up next to the snowman.

Amelia sized them up. "I can't tell."

Jasmine pulled the red hat from her head and plunked it onto the snowman. "There. Now he's definitely taller than your dad."

Both girls grinned at her.

Something warmed deep inside Sam. It felt good. And then he felt guilty. Here they were, laughing and joking and having fun, all without Kara. It shouldn't come so easily to him.

He could feel Jasmine's scrutiny.

"You girls must be hungry," she said, turning her attention to the girls. "I know I'm famished."

"I'm famished, too," Amelia said, obviously trying out the new word.

"Famished," Sophie agreed.

"Is Belle home?" Sam asked Jasmine.

Jasmine gave him an odd look. "Would she normally leave the girls here alone?"

"You were here." As he said the words, he realized it would be a huge imposition to expect Jasmine to babysit.

She paused before answering. "I appreciate the vote of confidence. But Belle's only just met me. I can't see her putting that kind of trust in a stranger."

Sam knew Jasmine was right. He also knew he wanted to trust her. He wasn't sure why, and it didn't make logical sense, but his instincts told him she would take good care of his daughters.

The girls trotted toward the side door into the house.

"You're right," Sam said. "Belle is very careful with the girls. And we wouldn't want to impose."

Jasmine shook her head. "It's no imposition at all. Your daughters are delightful. And, in any event, I'm the one imposing on you."

He knew he owed her an apology, and he wouldn't let himself walk away from that. "I was a boor last night. And I'm sorry. You're welcome to stay with us as long as you like."

"I understand this isn't the best time for you." She seemed to hesitate over her next words. "Belle told me about your wife."

He swallowed. "Yes. Well, it's been two years now."

Her tone was gentle. "Two years isn't such a long time."

He wasn't going to let himself dive into her sympathy. Two years was enough.

"You want your privacy," she said. "I'll try to respect that. If we're lucky, I'll be gone sometime tomorrow."

"Is that the forecast?" He was surprised. He hadn't heard an update since midday, but the snowfall didn't show any signs of letting up.

"That's my wishful thinking."

"Does the national weather service agree with you?"

"Not so far. But how long can something like this possibly last?"

Sam took in the steady fall of snowflakes, twinkling and magnified by the streetlights. "It's bound to end soon."

"And then my plane will come directly back to pick me up," she stated with determination.

"Is there a chance they won't?" he asked.

She looked startled. "No. Why would you ask that?"

"You sounded like you were giving yourself a pep talk."

"They'll come straight back," she stated with conviction. "They will absolutely come straight back."

Sam couldn't help but think Jasmine had to be treasured by her family and her friends. "Is there anyone—" He stopped himself before he could finish the question.

"Anyone what?"

"Nothing."

"Go ahead and ask."

He was just making polite conversation. Not asking now would be stranger than asking. "I was just wondering, besides your family, is there anyone waiting for you?"

The question seemed to put her on her guard. And she didn't answer.

"A boyfriend?" He clarified.

There was relief in her eyes. "Oh, no, nothing like that."

"What did you think I meant?"

"I was confused. I don't have a boyfriend."

He tried to imagine a universe in which men wouldn't be lining up to date her. "Are they intimidated by your father?"

A tiny smile twitched her lips. "You could say that."

"Well that's no fun. For you, I mean."

Her laugh was musical. He liked it.

"I'm used to it," she said.

"It's always been that way?"

"Let's say my social life has been somewhat limited by my circumstances."

"Locked up in an ivory tower?" he guessed.

"More than you can imagine."

Sam found his steps halting. He gazed up at Belle's big house, rising against the dark sky. It wasn't a tower and he wasn't trapped there. But Brock's lecture today had him thinking about how long he had imposed on Belle.

"Do you ever have the urge to escape?" he asked.

It took Jasmine a minute to speak. When she did, there was a touch of wonder to her tone. "Nobody's ever asked me that before."

"Because your life seems so fantastic?"

"A lot of people imagine they want to be me. They don't understand, of course. It's far more complicated than it looks."

"Who doesn't want to be rich?"

Her tone turned wistful. "Me sometimes." Then she seemed to catch herself. "I mean, there are days when I'm not sure I'm up to the task."

"I wouldn't want a lot of money." He admitted. "I want some. It's a necessity. I need to be able to provide for the girls, give them a few advantages, dance lessons, a good education, things like that."

"Being a good parent is probably the best thing you can

give them."

Sam knew she wasn't being critical. She didn't know him anywhere near well enough to judge him. But he felt the sting anyway. He wasn't a good parent right now. He was a mediocre parent.

"Amelia and Sophie adore you," Jasmine said.

He scoffed out a laugh. "Only because they don't have anything to compare me to."

She tilted her head sideways. "You don't mean that."

"Don't I?"

"If you do, you shouldn't."

Her hair was growing damp from the melting snowflakes. She had to be getting cold. He knew he should take her inside. He didn't know why he kept talking instead.

"They deserve more than me. They deserve…"

She reached out to touch his arm. Even though she wore a mitten and he wore a jacket, he felt the warmth of her touch permeate his skin. It was soothing.

"They've got you, Sam. Is life fair? Absolutely not. Do your girls deserve a mother? I would say yes. But that doesn't change reality."

"Reality sucks."

"It can."

Their gazes met and held, a connection gently pulsing between them. He wanted to step into it. With a start, he realized he wanted to draw her close, take her in his arms, kiss her deep, red lips.

He couldn't do that. He couldn't think that. He couldn't *want* that.

He withdrew from her touch, his tone gruffer than he'd intended. "We need to get inside."

Her gaze clouded. But she didn't say a word. Instead, she gracefully turned, walking away over the trampled snow.

He reached deep inside for a core of emotional strength, steadying himself before he followed.

JASMINE STARED AT the ceiling of guest room, its pale yellow panels accented by a narrow white crown molding. It was nearly two a.m., but she couldn't sleep. She couldn't forget the poignant expression on Sam's face outside in the yard, the pain in the depths of his brown eyes.

She was embarrassed by her own selfish feelings, the desire to sway toward him, a longing to lean in, be wrapped in his embrace. She was being greedy and unrealistic, but her arms felt empty. Her lips tingled with an unrequited kiss.

She turned sharply in the bed, adjusting the quilt around her shoulders for the hundredth time, determinedly closing her eyes and telling herself to go to sleep already.

Sam was an attractive man, sure. And there was nothing wrong with her experiencing romantic impulse. It was bound to happen eventually. Why not with a tall, handsome stranger? Sam didn't pussyfoot around. He said things to her that no man had ever dared. She felt edgy and excited in responding to him. His attitude made him seem strong and confident.

Was it any wonder she found the combination attractive? What she'd said to him was true. As heir to the throne, she couldn't date. Her formal dances with dignitaries in her own age group—few and far between—were the closest she'd ever come to a romantic encounter.

For a wild moment, she thought about taking this chance and kissing Sam.

She wondered how he'd react. But she knew how he'd react.

He wasn't interested in kissing Jasmine or anyone else. He was grieving for Kara.

Jasmine's next thought was that she needed to get home without delay. The longer she stayed in Tucker, the more complicated her life became. Even now, it was morning in Vollan, and her presence would be missed. The household would be up, breakfast over, the daily schedule posted in her office.

There would be a series of Christmas events planned for today, and she was letting people down by missing them. She knew they had prepared for months, and a royal guest brought attention to the concerts, parties, and fund-raisers.

Belle's guest room didn't have a phone, but she knew there was one in the kitchen. She'd tried several times during the day to call home, but the lines remained stubbornly dead. It had been embarrassing to realize, even if the lines had reconnected, she didn't know the palace phone number. She'd never had a need to memorize it. Her life was so strictly planned, no one had considered the possibility of her being stranded alone.

She hoped an operator could help her place the call.

She pulled back the covers and swung her feet to the floor. The nightgown Belle had lent her was a simple, cream-colored satin. She slipped into the matching robe that covered her arms and draped to mid-calf. The hallway carpet was soft on her feet, and the remnants of a fire in the living room kept the air temperature comfortable. The snow continued to swirl outside the windows, and the wind sounded like it was picking up.

Jasmine passed through the archway to the kitchen. She stopped short, seeing Sam at the breakfast bar, his arms folded on the countertop, head bowed down.

She knew she should leave him in peace, go back to her room without saying anything. But he looked exhausted and thoroughly dejected. She hesitated.

"Can't sleep?" he asked without looking up. Clearly he had heard her arrive.

"No," she answered. She swallowed. "You?"

He shook his head.

"I'll get out of your way."

He turned to look at her. "You were looking for something?"

"It's nothing important." There was also a phone in the

living room. She could try to call from there.

"What is it?" he asked.

"I was going to try to call home."

"Ah." He gestured to the telephone. "Be my guest."

"I can call from someplace else."

"You might as well see if it works." His gaze seemed to take in her outfit. His lips compressed in what looked like annoyance.

"I don't want to intrude."

He came to his feet. "Don't be ridiculous." He took three paces to the telephone counter and picked up the receiver.

He listened for a moment. Then shook his head. "Still out."

Jasmine sighed and her shoulders drooped.

"Sorry about that." He offered.

"It's not your fault."

He gestured to a bottle of brandy sitting on the breakfast bar. "Thirsty?"

She saw that he was drinking from a blown crystal snifter.

It was tempting.

"That hesitation is definitely not a no," he said, retrieving another snifter and returning to his chair. "It'll combat the jet lag."

She knew jet lag wasn't her problem. But the brandy might help her sleep.

"Thanks," she said.

He pulled out a second chair and gestured to it.

While she climbed up, he poured the brandy. She tightened the satin sash at her waist, making sure her neckline wasn't revealing cleavage.

He handed her the glass.

"I appreciate this," she said.

"Worried about your family?" he asked.

"Feeling guilty not being there."

She wasn't about to tell him her family wasn't her biggest problem in this moment. It was her wayward emotions. Sitting across from him, his worn t-shirt taut across his chest and broad shoulders, a pair of grey sweats riding low on his hips, her bare knees only inches from his, her attraction to him ramped up to new heights.

"What are you missing?" he asked.

"Christmas celebrations for the most part. I'd accepted a lot of invitations, and I hate backing out."

"Belle says the airport got a message to your plane. Surely people will understand."

"They'll be disappointed." As she said the words, she realized they made her sound conceited. Without knowing what she represented in Vollan, Sam would think she was full of her own self-importance. "What I mean to say, is that it's very rude."

He gave a little smirk. "I'm sure they will be disappointed. I bet you're the belle of the ball."

"Not in the way you think. It's all about my father. When I'm there, I represent him and the family." She didn't want to say too much, but she found she didn't want Sam to think poorly of her either.

"He must be a very important man."

"He has wide-ranging interests. When he can't be somewhere, people count on me to convey their messages to him. He helps out." She paused to better frame her answer. "With charitable donations, for example."

"I see."

"You can't sleep?" she asked in an effort to move the conversation away from herself.

She took a sip of the brandy while she waited for his answer.

He was silent for a long time.

"When I came into the yard," he finally said, speaking slowly, as though it was painful. "I saw those checkerboard pants. For the smallest of seconds, I thought you were Kara. I thought she'd come back, that a miracle had happened, or that it had all been a mix-up."

Jasmine's stomach clenched with regret. "I had no idea."

"That they were hers? Of course you didn't. How could you?"

"They were dress-up clothes."

"I always hated those pants." He threw back a swallow of the brandy. "She liked them, but she stopped wearing them a long time ago and gave them to the girls for play."

Jasmine didn't know what to say. She never would have put them on if she'd known they could hurt Sam.

"But I should thank you," he said.

"What for?" The question was surprised right out of her.

"Kara is gone. I knew that. I've known it intellectually for a long time. But tonight I discovered what was holding me back." His gaze trapped hers.

"What?" Jasmine asked in a quiet voice.

"I need to understand it emotionally as well." His stark honesty touched her. "I don't know how to do that yet. But I do know I have to try. I have to try much harder."

"That's admirable," Jasmine said.

"I haven't done anything yet."

"It's a start."

"We'll see."

They fell silent.

His fingers drummed on the marble countertop.

Hers curled into her palms. She didn't know what to do with the rush of emotion that flushed her skin and made her lips tingle like she'd tasted hot peppers. The urge to kiss him was back in force.

His hair was mussed, his face unshaven, and his eyes were dark as espresso.

Her lips parted.

His breathing stopped, and the air around them seemed to crackle with expectation.

She reached for his hand, but he snapped it away.

"I'm sorry about the phones," he said. Then he downed the rest of his drink.

Now she flushed with embarrassment. What had she been thinking in trying to touch him?

"I knew it was a long shot." She managed, trying hard to keep her voice normal.

"They'll reconnect eventually." He drew back in his chair.

She wondered if she should leave. There was no way she could down the remains of her brandy, so she took as big a swallow as she dared.

"Has this happened before?" she asked, trying to alleviate the tension between them.

"Not for about ten years." He was clearly willing to do his part to try to bring things back to normal.

"Did you live there then?"

"I was born here."

"That must be nice, to know all your neighbors." She was making silly small talk. But she didn't know what else to do.

"Did you move a lot as a child?" he asked.

Jasmine thought of the palace. Twelve generations of the Arcelus family had lived there.

"No."

"Small town?" he asked.

"Small city. Roxen Canal."

"Do you like it there?"

She found herself smiling at the thought of the capital. "I love it there. It's chock full of history and art. We have museums and theatres, parks and green space. Everyone skates on the canal in winter. And we have the most modern rapid transit system in northern Europe."

"You sound like a tourism commercial."

Jasmine felt her cheeks warm again. "I don't mean to."

"It's okay. I liked it. It sounds wonderful."

"It is wonderful."

"I hope you get back there soon."

"Me, too." She did.

So many things were waiting for her. So many things needed her attention. But for this small moment in time, she found herself glad to be in Sam's kitchen, sipping brandy. It didn't make sense, but it was strangely restful to be trapped here within the whirling snow and have the world move on without her.

Chapter Four

"LOOK HOW DEEP it is *now*!" Amelia's excited voice traveled from the living room to the kitchen where Jasmine was eating pancakes with Belle.

Sam had left for work early, only mobile because of the snowplow blade fixed to the front of his truck.

Jasmine didn't share Amelia's excitement. The local radio station was reporting three feet of snow with no letup in sight. A state of emergency had been declared from Maine to New Jersey. Airports were closed, roads were impassible, communications were offline, and areas were experiencing wide power outages.

"Mr. Snowman is buried," Sophie sang.

"The hat," Jasmine said to Belle, regretting that she'd left it outside.

"What hat?"

"I left the red hat on the snowman's head last night."

Belle laughed at that. "I guess we'll find it in the spring."

"We need to decorate the tree," Sophie said, sliding into the kitchen on her sock feet. "It's dry by now." She skipped over to the counter and helped herself to a plate.

Amelia appeared, giving Belle a pointed look, obviously trying to remind her about the decorations at Sam's house.

"We'll see what your father says about the tree," Belle said.

Amelia sidled up to her. "What about the decorations?" she whispered while Sophie took a couple of pancakes from the warmer on the stove.

Jasmine had never experienced a more relaxed and chaotic method of dining. It was odd, but not unpleasant. For the most part, Belle cooked, put the prepared breakfast food on the counter or the stove, and everyone randomly grazed their way through it.

Belle spoke to Amelia. "You both have lessons today, and I promised to help at the church."

"Maybe Daddy could—"

"I didn't get a chance to talk to your Daddy yet."

Amelia compressed her lips.

"Get yourself some pancakes," said Belle, giving Amelia a rub on the shoulder.

Amelia looked dejected, but did as she was asked.

"Where's the raspberry syrup?" Sophie asked.

"Bottom shelf in the fridge door," Belle answered.

"Was that about the homemade decorations?" Jasmine asked Belle, remembering Amelia's earlier concern about Sophie.

Belle gave a nod. "She's not wrong. But I'm afraid of Sam's reaction to the idea."

"You don't want to ask him." Jasmine understood. Even though she now knew Sam was trying to work through it, his sensitivity to his wife's death was still acute.

"I don't want to make a big deal about it. If I had time, I'd walk to the house and get them. The girls could quietly hang them on the tree. They'd likely blend right in. That way, Sophie feels like she's having more of a traditional Christmas, but we're not throwing it up in Sam's face."

"Is the house far away?"

"A little over two miles."

Jasmine made up her mind quickly. "I could do it for you."

Belle looked surprised. "Through the snow?"

"We found some boots that fit me last night. It'll save me from doing nothing but check on the phone lines all day long." Jasmine liked the idea of getting outside and having something useful to do.

"I could give you my key." Belle was obviously warming to the idea.

"Can you give me directions?" Jasmine asked. "Maybe draw me a map."

"It's easy," said Belle. "You walk down to Main Street then follow Main up to Green Place. It's two blocks in, the house with twin oaks at the end of the driveway."

"Do you know where I'd find the decorations?" Jasmine was hesitant about going into Sam's house, but she wasn't about to back out.

"They're in the green and blue cupboard," Amelia said.

Jasmine suddenly realized Amelia and Sophie were hanging on every word.

Belle looked surprised to realize it, but her expression quickly recovered. "At the bottom of the basement stairs?" she asked.

"Daddy moved it to the playroom," Sophie said. Her blue eyes were big and hopeful. "Are you getting my decorations?"

Jasmine could see this was important to Sophie. "I'm going to try." She assured her. "Where's the playroom?"

"Down the basement stairs," Amelia said with breathless enthusiasm. She balanced her pancakes as she walked toward the table. "You go past the laundry room and turn. The green and blue cupboard is beside the ping-pong table."

"Under the window," Sophie added. "Can you get our stockings?"

Jasmine looked to Belle. She didn't want to disappoint Sophie, but she didn't want to upset Sam either.

"Mommy made the stockings," Amelia said.

"Let's pick them up," Belle said diplomatically. "We'll decide later if we should hang them or use the ones we made last year. I really loved the ones you made for yourselves."

The girls looked at each other as if seeking mutual reassurance. Their longing was clear, and Jasmine's sympathy went out to them. She had to wonder if Sam realized what a burden he was putting on his daughters.

"Okay," they said simultaneously.

"Eat your pancakes," said Belle. "The only way to get anywhere today is by walking, so you're going to need some extra energy."

Jasmine finished her own breakfast, dressed in more borrowed clothing and set off on the walk to Sam's house.

From what she could see that wasn't buried or obscured by the falling snow, Tucker was a beautiful, little town. The yards were large, the houses pretty, many of them with Christmas decorations shining through the gloom.

Main Street had been plowed, but the side streets were all buried in snow. And the snow was knee deep on the sidewalks, dampening her pants and creeping into the tops of her boots. But her hands were warm in the knit mittens, and the hood from her jacket kept the snowflakes off her hair. And the air was crisp and fresh, with the world unnaturally quiet around her.

She experienced the same peace she'd felt in the patch of woods beside the airport. She might be stranded, but her worries were also far way, across the ocean, and there was nothing she could do about her real life right now. It could have upset her, but instead she was enjoying the respite.

It was difficult to read the street signs since they were covered in snow. But she managed to navigate her way to Green Place. She watched the house numbers, growing ever closer to Sam's. Then she spotted the twin oak trees, and she knew she'd been successful.

The driveway was blown in, and it was even deeper than the sidewalks. She fought her way toward the covered porch, stumbling partway and falling into the soft snow. She couldn't help but laugh at her clumsiness. Then she couldn't help but imagine what Darren would say to her predicament. He wouldn't laugh, that was for sure. He'd tell her it was undignified. It was, but she didn't care. There was nobody here to see her.

"Can I help you?" A woman's voice came from behind.

Startled by the abrupt intrusion, Jasmine swiftly came to her feet and brushed herself off. "I'm fine," she called, turning to see a dark haired woman in a bright purple ski jacket.

She looked to be about thirty. She was slim and short, and was having just as much trouble as Jasmine navigating the snow.

"Are you looking for Sam Cutler?"

"You know Sam?" Jasmine asked. She hadn't counted on anyone seeing her here, especially someone who might report back to Sam.

"Yes," said the woman, making it to Jasmine. She was pretty, looking very fresh-faced and open.

"Belle sent me," Jasmine said. She fished into her jacket pocket for Belle's key to prove the claim. "She needed something picked up."

"Are you the woman who got stranded?"

Jasmine peeled off her glove and offered her hand. "I am.

I'm Jasmine."

"I heard about you. I'm Melanie Montrose." The woman shook Jasmine's hand. "I live next door."

"It's a pleasure to meet you, Melanie," Jasmine said.

"You walked over?" Melanie glanced around, obviously checking to see if she'd missed a vehicle.

"It seems to be the only way to get around today. Belle took the girls downtown for their lessons."

Melanie gestured to the house next door. "Good for Belle. My kids are going stir-crazy in there."

"How many children do you have?"

"Three. My daughter Libby is very close to the twins. They were inseparable until…well…"

"Belle told me about Kara," Jasmine said softly.

Melanie's expression clouded. "It was a tragedy."

"I can't even imagine."

"My husband Brock has been working on Sam, trying to help him heal, but it's a long process." Melanie drew in a deep breath. "It's good that you're getting something from the house. Dare I hope it's to do with Christmas?"

"It is." Jasmine decided to take a chance on bringing Melanie into her confidence. "But Sam doesn't know about it. The girls really wanted some special decorations for the tree. Belle thinks it's a good idea, but she doesn't seem sure how to broach it with Sam."

"That's understandable. Brock has tried everything he knows. He's getting ready to push harder."

"He sounds like a good friend."

"Can I offer you some tea?" Melanie asked. "It'll be a long, cold walk back. If it would help, I've got a small backpack at the house you could use to carry the decorations." She glanced down at Jasmine's snowy clothes. "And I think we can come up with some dry socks."

"You're incredibly kind." Jasmine couldn't help but wonder if there was any end to the hospitality of Tucker's citizens.

FOR THE FIRST time in months, Sam had left his shop early. He'd meant what he said to Jasmine last night. It was time for him to move forward. Christmas might be the worst possible time for him to make that decision, but there was nothing he could do about the calendar.

He plowed his way to his own driveway, parking at the side of the road. The sun was going down, and visibility was poor, but he could see footprints in the snow leading to his front porch.

He shut off the truck and left the vehicle. Even with the trail to follow, it was slow going. Snow clung to the fronts of his pants. He stomped on the concrete of the porch, glancing around to see if anything had been disturbed. Everything seemed normal, he assumed there'd been a delivery attempt, or Brock may have been checking on the house earlier this morning. His car was gone now.

He retrieved his key, staring at it for a long time before sliding it into the lock. He braced himself for the familiar sights, sounds and smells of his house. He knew this was going to hurt, but he also knew he had to do it.

The key turned easily, too easily, especially considering the temperature. The front door lock always stuck in the cold. It felt like the door was already unlocked.

Sam went on alert. He silently turned the door handle, pushing in, opening it halfway, knowing the hinge had a squeak past that. At least it used to have a squeak at that point. Not taking any chances, he moved sideways through the narrow opening.

There, he paused, listening carefully. Brock and Melanie's cars were both gone, so it couldn't be either of them.

He heard it—footsteps in the hall.

Anger overran his fear. How dare somebody break into his house? If it was vandals, he was hauling them off to the police station.

He marched forward, shoulders squared, ready to take on whoever it was.

He rounded the corner and nearly ran straight into a short figure. They had a pack slung over one shoulder, and let out a high pitched squeak of shock.

He grasped them by the upper arms, immediately realizing it was a woman.

"*What* do you think you're doing?" He shouted.

"Sam?"

He jerked back to focus. "Jasmine?"

"You scared me half to death."

He didn't think he could be more shocked. "What is this? Why are you here?"

Her presence made no sense at all.

"I didn't expect you," she said.

"Are you stealing something?" It occurred to him that both he and Belle might have been far too quick to trust Jasmine.

"Belle sent me."

Sam didn't believe that for a second. Belle had no reason to send Jasmine to his house. Belle was completely respectful of his privacy.

"Nice try," he said. "Tell me the truth."

Fear crossed her expression. "That *is* the truth."

He realized he still had a hold of her, but he wasn't about to let her go until he knew what was going on.

"What's in the bag?" he demanded.

She hesitated, her eyes going wide.

"If you don't answer, I'm going to take it from you."

"Sam, please."

He reached for the backpack.

She jerked back, trying to protect it.

"Jewelry?" he asked. "Money?" Not that he could re-member leaving any amount of cash in the house.

"*Nothing.*"

"It's not nothing."

The claim was preposterous. She'd broken into his house and was leaving with a backpack full of something. He reached for the pack again, this time getting a firm grasp on it.

There was a momentary tug of war, but she must have quickly realized she was no match for him. She let it go.

"Be careful," she begged. "It might break."

He unzipped the top.

"Sam, I'm so sorry."

"Sorry you tried to steal from me, or sorry you got caught?" He pulled the pack open, staring inside.

Then his breath caught in his throat, and the fight drained right out of him. Staring up was a picture of Kara. He could almost hear her voice, smell her perfume.

"Sophie wanted them," Jasmine told him in a regretful voice. "They weren't sure how to ask you. Belle gave me her key."

He steeled his emotions, pressing the two halves of the zipper together. "You shouldn't have done this."

"I didn't expect to see you here."

"What else did you see?"

"What?"

"Did you snoop around? Look in the other rooms? What else did you find out about me while you were here?"

"Nothing."

"I don't believe you."

What were the odds that she'd gone straight to the basement and back? The basement door was straight across from the master bedroom. She would have seen it. She had to have seen it.

He suddenly knew he had to get it over with. He had to do what he'd come to do and he had to do it right now.

He dropped the pack to the floor, marching around her, bee-lining down the hall. The master bedroom door was closed, but that didn't mean a thing. Without giving himself time to think, he grasped the handle, turned it and pushed it open.

The sight hit him like a freight train. He all but staggered under the force.

It was exactly how he remembered it—the upturned bed, the broken lamp, the torn paintings, scattered books and clothing, and the jagged hole in the wall.

"Sam?" Jasmine's voice sounded small beside him.

He braced himself on the doorjamb, squeezing hard.

"What happened?" she asked.

"I happened." He forced himself to look at the mess. "I had a bad day. I was upset."

"Has it been like this…"

He struggled for breath. "For a very long time."

He focused on a landscape painting sitting crooked against the dresser. He clearly remembered smashing it over the bedpost. The quilt was crumpled in the corner. He'd torn a pillow in half, and feathers were scattered. Odd that he didn't remember that part. Some moments were crystal clear, while other moments were a complete blank.

"This is what's kept you away," Jasmine said, her voice barely a breath.

It was more than this room that had kept him away. But it was definitely his frenzy here that had driven him away in the first place. He'd been trying to hold it together back then. He'd thought he was holding it together.

But Kara's slippers had set him off. The smallest of things, but one day seeing them side by side beneath the bed had reminded him of everything he'd lost. He put his fist through the wall, and the floodgates had opened. His heart beat hard and fast with the horrible memory.

Luckily, the girls had been visiting Libby.

"I'm not proud of this," he told Jasmine.

She touched his arm. He flinched, but he didn't pull away. He let the warmth of human contact seep into his skin.

"It's not your fault," she said.

"It's absolutely my fault."

"You were in pain."

He had been. He'd been in excruciating pain that night, wracked with guilt for letting Kara drive. He was still in pain now, though it wasn't as acute. It was moderated, dulled by time.

He tried to mentally measure the difference. It was definitely better, but he couldn't say by how much. He knew he wouldn't lose it again and trash something else. He'd at least come that far.

"Would it help?" She seemed to hesitate. "Would it help if I straightened up for you?"

"*No!*"

She flinched under his shout and he clamped his jaw shut.

Brock had offered more than once to help, repair the hole in the wall. He was the only person besides Sam who knew about the breakdown. At least, he knew about part of the breakdown. He knew Sam had put his fist through the wall, but he thought it had stopped at that.

Now, Sam stared at the room, knowing it was his responsibility to clean it up. He asked himself how he'd do that. If he could make himself cross the threshold, where would he begin?

"Why did you come here today?" Jasmine asked.

He dragged his gaze from the disaster to look at her. His heart rate decelerated, and some of the tension left his shoulders.

He wanted to be honest with her along with himself. "I'm here because it's time."

"You shouldn't do this alone," she said. "You shouldn't have come here alone."

"I have to do this alone."

"You have friends."

"You think I want my friends to see this?"

"Then let me help instead."

Before he could bark out another refusal, she continued speaking. "I'm a stranger, Sam. After this week, you're never going to see me again." Her roving gaze took in the room. "Maybe there's value in the separation between us."

It was an astonishing offer. He couldn't believe he was considering it.

What was there about Jasmine that made her seem safe? Something in his subconscious seemed to want him to trust her. If he hadn't felt some kind of deep-seated trust, he wouldn't have opened the bedroom door while she was in the house.

"If you had to start today," she asked, "what would you do? What's the first thing you'd move?"

"Why did you ask it that way?" He was wondering the same thing himself. It was strange to be on such a similar wavelength.

"Even the most monumental tasks start with a single action," she said. "They start with a single step, the smallest of movements forward."

"The bookshelf," he said, making up his mind. "I'd pick up the bookshelf."

It was face down in the middle of the room, blocking almost everything else.

"Good choice."

"You're talking to me like I'm five years old."

"I'll help. Let's break the ice. Nothing but the bookshelf. After that, if you want to stop, we'll stop."

He knew she was handling him. But he also didn't hate it. For the first time since that night, he could actually think about entering his old bedroom.

"Okay," he said.

"You will?" She seemed surprised, but she quickly recovered. "Do you want to go first?"

"Yes."

He gathered his strength and took a step forward. Just like that, he was in the room. And he discovered his emotions were manageable. He took another step, and then another. And then he was at the bookshelf and he gasped a corner.

She was right there with him, taking hold of the opposite corner. As they lifted, the remaining books fell out, clattering to pile on the floor. They carried the shelf to its proper place against the wall and set it down.

Their gazes met.

Although the same question had to be on both of their minds, she didn't ask.

He gave himself a minute, focusing on her instead of the room around him.

And then he was ready, more ready than he could have imagined.

"We can pick up the books," he said.

She smiled, and it gave him a new rush of strength.

SAM STOPPED HIS truck in Belle's driveway. Snowflakes drifted down outside, and the pack of Christmas decorations sat on the bench seat between them. He shut off the engine, palming the keys. But he didn't move to open the door.

Instead, he angled his body toward Jasmine.

"I don't want them to know," he said.

She waited.

"About the bedroom. They haven't been inside the house since it happened."

"Belle?" Jasmine asked.

Sam shook his head. "If she'd seen that mess, she would have said something." He gave a raw, pained chuckle. "Or maybe had me locked up."

"You don't need to be locked up."

What Sam needed was to heal. And to do that, he needed to move ahead with his life. Today was a start, and she was gratified to have helped in any small way. But there was a lot more work for him to do.

"Do you mind keeping this between us?" he asked.

She reflexively reached out to cover his hand. "I'll absolutely keep it between us. Your secret's not mine to share, Sam."

"I appreciate that."

His hand was cool beneath hers. His skin was tough and callused, strong and yet strangely vulnerable. She found herself closing her grip.

He shut his eyes and she was overwhelmed by the urge to

put her arms around him. If anyone was in need of simple human comfort, it was Sam in this moment. But she didn't dare. He was still wrapped up in the loss of his wife, and her feelings were a complex mix of sympathy, compassion, and desire. She'd be a fool to act on any of them.

"How do you want to explain being together?" she asked.

"That I picked you up on the road." He looked uncertain, as if he was worried how she'd react to the magnitude of the lie.

"We can say that."

She let his hand go and he flexed it.

Then she patted the backpack. "And these? Do you want to pretend you didn't see them? The girls were going to secretly hang them at the back of the tree."

Now his hands clenched the steering wheel. "They don't have to do that."

"They're trying to protect you."

"I should be protecting them."

"You are protecting them. You've kept them at Belle's all this time."

"Is that what you see?"

"I see a father who loves his daughters and is struggling to put their lives back together."

"I thought you'd have seen a crazy man who was falling down on his responsibilities."

Jasmine found herself smiling at his characterization. It was probably harsh, but likely not entirely untrue. "I think your instincts to push forward are good."

"I know they are."

Her heart went out to him for the tragedy he'd had to accept. "I'm sorry."

"It's not your fault."

"I'm still sorry."

He held her gaze for a long time, and she felt her pulse leap and her heart flutter helplessly in her chest. Nothing could come of these feelings. She'd be back home before she knew it, and this moment would be a distant memory. But it was still an exhilarating sensation, and she allowed herself to absorb it for a few more seconds.

Sam was an extraordinary man, harsh on himself, yet tender and loving to the people around him. She'd never met anyone like him, never interacted in such a raw and honest way.

"We should go inside," he said, voice gruff.

"The girls will be waiting." She told herself to move.

"Thank you for this."

"There's nothing to thank me for."

"There's a lot to thank you for." He took hold of the backpack and opened his door.

Jasmine followed suit, climbing carefully down into the slippery snow. She was sad to have the intimacy end, but she followed him up the walkway and into a side door that led to the laundry room and Sam's real life.

Amelia and Sophie scampered into the doorway, bumping into each other.

"Daddy." Amelia's tone was breathless, then a confused look came over her face. "You're with Jasmine." She was clearly trying to figure out the implications, obviously wondering if they were in some kind of trouble.

"I met her on the way here," Sam said in a hearty voice. He held up the backpack. "She says she brought you something."

"Did you find them?" Sophie asked Jasmine, glancing hesitantly to her father, clearly trying to gauge his mood.

"I found them," Jasmine said.

Belle arrived. She stilled, and her eyes widened on the backpack in Sam's hand.

Sam spoke to her. "I hear the girls wanted some Christmas decorations."

Belle's anxious gaze darted to Jasmine.

"Sam picked me up," Jasmine said. "I showed him what I was bringing back."

"Shall I bring in the tree?" Sam asked his girls, a smile on his face as he made an obvious attempt to move the conversation to safer territory.

"Can we?" Amelia asked, her expression immediately clearing.

"The tree, the tree," Sophie called out.

"I have spaghetti on the stove," Belle said. "We can eat first and then decorate."

"Sounds delicious," Sam said, locating a pair of leather

gloves. "I'll set up the tree while you dish up dinner."

Jasmine couldn't help but be impressed with how well he was pulling this off. There was no trace of the emotions he'd coped with back in his old bedroom. He was a great actor.

"Do you need some help?" she asked him.

"Can you hold the doors?"

"I can do that." She knew it was cold in the garage, so she re-zipped her coat.

"You girls move the plants from the bay window and make a space," he told his daughters.

They immediately trotted for the living room.

"Be careful," he called behind them. "Don't spill the dirt."

"Sam," Belle said gently, moving toward him, a questioning expression on her face. "Are you okay with this?"

"I'm fine with it," he told her.

She looked skeptical.

"They're just tree ornaments. The girls should have them for Christmas."

She watched him a moment longer and then gave a nod.

He settled his hands in the battered gloves and opened the door that led to the garage.

Jasmine followed him down three concrete stairs. The air was cool in the big open space, with darkness showing beyond the three small windows on the back wall. Belle's red compact car was parked in one stall; the other two stalls were filled with shelving, benches, tools, and storage boxes.

The tree was at the far end, propped up in a painted red stand, its broad, bushy branches extending out.

"It's beautiful," Jasmine said as they came to a stop in front of it.

Jasmine had never decorated a Christmas tree herself. The festivities in the palace were carefully planned, crafted, and organized by the staff. Each year, they chose a theme. It might be snowmen or angels, Santa's workshop, or simply a color scheme. Last year everything had been done in gold and white. It was crisp and clean, but incredibly elegant.

"Beautiful." Sam echoed, an odd inflection in his voice.

She turned and realized he was looking at her and not the tree. She felt her cheeks warm in reaction.

"Did you know you're beautiful?" he asked.

She had no idea how to respond to that.

"Of course you know you're beautiful."

She looked down at her utilitarian outfit. She couldn't say she felt beautiful at the moment. She was slightly sweaty. Her hair was a mess from the walk and the wind. And she hadn't worn makeup in days.

"I haven't noticed a beautiful woman in a very long time," he said in a quiet tone.

He removed his glove and reached slowly up to touch her cheek.

She couldn't stop herself from leaning into his palm.

"So smooth." There was a reverence in his tone.

He dipped his head, putting his lips against her hair. She

couldn't call it a kiss, more a tender, intimate touch. She reveled in its power, closing her eyes to memorize every nuance of the moment.

He drew back slowly. She did, too. They gazed into each other's eyes.

"Daddy?" Amelia's voice jolted them back to reality.

The garage door opened.

"Where are you?" she called. "What's taking so long?"

Sam took a step back, focusing his attention on the tree. "We're on our way."

Jasmine blinked herself back to reality. She tried to bring her emotions under control. But they didn't want to be controlled.

They wanted Sam.

Chapter Five

WATCHING JASMINE STRING a final garland across the tree, Sam could still feel the silk of her cheek against his hand. Her breath had been soft puffs against him. Her skin was warm to his touch. While the sweet scent of her hair fanned around him.

He tried to tell himself it was only human comfort. He'd had an emotional day, and something about Jasmine soothed him.

She stepped back from the tree now to survey her work.

"Can we put the star on top?" Amelia asked.

"It's Sophie's turn this year," Belle said.

"I know it's Sophie's turn. I'm going to get it out of the box."

"Will you pick me up, Daddy?" asked Sophie, squaring herself to the tree and presenting him with her back.

Amelia brought over the etched, silver star, handing it carefully to her sister. Excitement shone in both of their eyes.

He was aware of Belle's watchfulness and of Jasmine moving to an armchair to sit down. He wondered if Jasmine was remembering his caress. She hadn't backed away. If anything, she'd leaned in.

He was ready to admit that touching her was like coming out of dormancy. He was still a man, still human, and though he might not be proud of his needs, they existed, and he wasn't going to be able to ignore them forever.

He mentally packed his newfound acceptance away. It was something to explore later, when he was alone and had time to think.

"Ready?" he asked Sophie, wrapping his hands around her waist to hoist her up to the tree.

He waited for the ache of loneliness to pressurize his chest, like it always did when he was reminded of family moments with Kara.

"I'm ready," Sophie said.

He lifted her to sit on his shoulders. She gripped his head, wobbling a little as he slowly rose.

"Whoa," she called. "This is really high."

Strangely, his ache was muted.

"Closer, Daddy, closer," Amelia called.

"You're going to have to reach for it," he told Sophie.

He felt her lean and tightened his grip on her thighs. "I've got you." He inched between two of the lower branches, careful not to brush off any ornaments.

"Up, up," Amelia called encouragingly from the floor.

Jasmine stood, seeming to move for a better angle. Sam tried to ignore her, but he couldn't. He was hyperaware of her movement toward him, the distance between them, his desire to have her come closer so he could touch her again.

"Did it!" Sophie cried with delight. Then she gasped as she canted sideways, flailing her arms.

Jasmine surged forward, reaching up for her.

"I've got her," Sam said, but momentum carried Jasmine's chest up against him, her soft breasts molding against his side.

His muscles contracted and his heart rate all but doubled.

"Help me down," Sophie called out, reaching for Jasmine.

Jasmine was laughing as she moved in front of him. "Give me your arms," she said to Sophie.

Sophie reached down to grasp Jasmine's outstretched arms. Jasmine's movements increased the intimacy of their touch and a surge of energy buzzed through his skin.

Sophie laughed, and Jasmine smiled, and Sam couldn't help but smile in return. Amelia jumped on his back, obviously anxious to get in on the fun.

Something flashed, and he realized Belle was taking a picture. It would be a happy Christmas picture without Kara. He instantly sobered. He moved Amelia aside and came to his feet, backing away from the little group.

"It looks very nice," he said, struggling to keep the enthusiasm in his tone.

Jasmine obviously sensed something in him and looked up.

"Come on, girls," Belle said cheerfully. "Help me make some hot cocoa."

"With mini marshmallows?" Amelia asked.

"With mini marshmallows." Belle confirmed. "I think we've all earned it."

Jasmine watched the trio leave for the kitchen. "She's very observant."

"Amelia?"

"Belle. She cares a lot about you."

Sam forced himself to put some distance between them, making a show of looking at the tree from all angles. It had tiny white lights, glass ornaments of all shapes and sizes, silver garland, and strings of cranberries. His gaze went to Kara's picture, shellacked onto the ornament Amelia had made in grade two. There'd once been one of him as well, but it had long since been lost.

"Have you checked the phone lines since dinner?" he asked Jasmine, reminding himself she was leaving soon.

"They're still down. I'm going to walk down to city hall tomorrow and see if there's anything more to find out."

"I've never seen a storm last this long." He focused on the snow falling under the streetlights.

"On the radio, they're calling it a hundred-year storm."

"Do you get snow in Vollan?"

"We do." She said. Her voice was even. There was no sign that their touch had affected her as it had him. "Not too much in the capital, but up in the mountains it can get quite deep."

"Your family must be getting frustrated."

"I'm fairly certain the pilot got the radio message. Not that it would be hard to figure out that I was stranded in Tucker. It's not like I could have left the plane at any other point on the journey."

She was making a joke and he found himself smiling again.

He found himself curious about Jasmine's life in Vollan. "You said you were missing Christmas events. What are they?"

"So far, I've missed a concert or two, probably a play" she said. "The official lighting of the tree in the city's square. There's a children's party that I usually attend."

"You don't have any children of your own." He knew that, and he wondered what would bring her to a children's party.

"Some of my friends have children. And I love watching their faces when Santa shows up."

"You want kids someday?" He couldn't help but think she'd be a good mother.

Amelia and Sophie certainly liked her. And she seemed patient and intuitive. As a stranger, it was fairly incredible that she'd offered to walk two miles in the snow to retrieve Christmas ornaments for his girls.

"Definitely," she said. "Someday. I'll have to get married first."

For some reason, her expression turned pensive, as if the thought of a husband was disagreeable.

"You don't want to get married?"

"It's hard to imagine."

"Why?"

"When you haven't met anybody suitable…"

"*Suitable?*" He found it an odd choice of words.

"That's the right…" She hesitated. "I don't know…"

Now she had him curious. "Are you looking for something specific in a husband?'

"I guess what I mean is, how do you know if somebody is right?"

"I'm not the guy to ask about that." He'd never had to consider a woman from the perspective of whether or not she'd make a suitable partner.

"You found Kara," Jasmine said. "You obviously figured out she was right for you."

"I found Kara when I was seven years old." He could still remember riding his two-wheeler bike along Green Drive and seeing her drawing with chalk on the sidewalk. "We grew up together. We started seriously dating at sixteen. It never occurred to me that it could be anyone else."

"I envy that." And then she seemed to realize what she had said. "I'm sorry, I didn't mean—"

"I know what you meant. Kara and I were lucky. I can't say I know how other people do it."

"It's complicated for me."

He could guess why. "Because of your rich, overprotective father?"

"Truth is." She looked distinctly self-conscious as she spoke. "I've never been on a real date."

Sam couldn't hide his surprise. "How is that possible?" Again, he couldn't imagine the men weren't lining up for the opportunity to take her out. "How old are you?"

"Twenty-four."

There was no way, no way in the world that she hadn't had hundreds of offers.

"You must have gone to college," he said.

"I have a degree in international studies."

"And?" He prompted. Didn't they date at colleges in Vollan?

"I attended close to home. So, no dorm life. No frat parties. No post-football keggers."

"I'm starting to feel sorry for you." And trying to imagine how a European country could be so different from America. "They have football in Vollan?"

"You'd call it soccer. But, yes, we have a very accomplished professional team in the European league." Her answer betrayed pride.

"Are you a fan?" he asked.

"I'm a fan of everything Vollan does."

"Patriotic. I admire that."

"I am extraordinarily patriotic. My country is everything to me."

"I wish I could help you get home," he said, trying to mean it.

But he knew he didn't mean it. At least not in this moment. He wanted her to stay right here in Tucker. She was beginning to fascinate him, and he wanted the snow to keep falling and the airport to remain closed so she had no choice but to stay.

JASMINE COULDN'T HELP but feel proud of the Christmas tree. It wasn't her accomplishment alone, not by any stretch. But she had contributed. And it was a beautiful tree. And this morning she sat sipping her coffee gazing up at it against the backdrop of the snowy world outside.

"We need to buy some presents," Amelia said, joining Jasmine, still clad in a pair of yellow pajamas. "Then we can wrap them and put them under the tree. It'll look even prettier then."

"Won't Santa Claus take care of that?" Jasmine asked.

Sophie came in from the kitchen. "We're too old to believe in Santa Claus."

The two girls took up opposite ends of the sofa. Jasmine was curled in a big armchair.

"We believe in shopping malls," Amelia said with an almost comical air of worldliness.

"I want to get Daddy a basketball," Sophie said.

"That would be interesting to wrap," Jasmine said.

"He never shoots hoops anymore," Amelia said. "He used to shoot hoops with Brock. When we lived next door."

"There's lots of things Daddy doesn't do anymore," Sophie said, a wistfulness to her tone.

Once again, Jasmine's heart went out to the girls. She wasn't sure what to say to comfort them. She knew they didn't need comfort from her. They needed Sam to be whole again so he could enthusiastically participate in every part of their lives. She wished there was something she could do to speed up the process.

"I wish we could have the party," Sophie said on a sigh.

"The party was Daddy's favorite all time thing," Amelia said.

"A basketball party?" Jasmine asked.

"No, silly," Amelia said. "The *Christmas* party. Everyone would help, and everyone would come. It was awesome."

"Everyone from school," Sophie said. "All our friends."

"It was a school party?" Jasmine asked.

"Grown-ups, too. We'd sweep out the warehouse. It was the only place big enough that was free. Then we'd set up tables and a stage. We had games and songs and balloons."

"And bubbles," Amelia chimed in. "We'd always blow bubbles. Remember, Sophie?"

Amelia mimicked bubble blowing, and Sophie pretended to bat them out of the air.

"At a warehouse?" Jasmine asked.

"Daddy's warehouse. It used to have wood and stuff in it.

But the business changed, and it hasn't changed back."

"Oh." Now Jasmine understood why they couldn't have the party. The last thing Sam would want to do was be at the helm of a traditional town Christmas party. She could only imagine Kara must have taken a pivotal role in the event.

"I wish we could do it again," Sophie said.

"The kids all miss it," Amelia said.

"I bet Daddy would like it," Sophie said.

"He liked the tree." Amelia gazed up at the sparkling tree.

Sophie followed suit. "And he didn't mind us getting the old decorations."

"He seemed really happy last night," Amelia said.

"I like it when Daddy laughs."

Jasmine liked it when Sam laughed, too. She wasn't in a position to judge, but she thought he'd seemed happier last night, more relaxed than he'd been since her arrival. She had to wonder if the few minutes he'd spent in his old bedroom had helped break the ice. Maybe he was ready to start moving on with his life.

She'd be happy for him if he was.

"Maybe you could ask him." She suggested to the girls.

Sophie slid closer to Amelia. "He'd just say no."

"He might not." Jasmine was far from convinced Sam would say yes, but she found she didn't want to dash the girls' hopes before it was necessary.

"We could surprise him," Amelia said. "He'll like it if he

sees it. I know he will."

Red flags went off in Jasmine's brain. She could only imagine the ways Amelia's idea could go wrong.

"Can we, Grandma? Can we?" Sophie asked.

Jasmine turned to see Belle come into the living room.

"Can we what?" Belle asked in a cheerful voice. She also seemed more relaxed than usual after the tree decorating.

"Surprise Daddy," Amelia said.

"Surprise him how?"

"With a party. The party."

"*The* party," Sophie added.

"The Christmas party?" Belle asked, looking as worried as Jasmine felt.

"He'll like it," Amelia said, coming to her feet. "I know he will."

Belle's voice grew gentle. "I know how much you girls love that party."

"*Everybody* loves the party," Sophie said, bouncing to her feet beside her sister. "Every single body in the *whole town* loves the party. It's the town's party."

Belle gave Jasmine a helpless look. "It's true."

"We'll do *everything*," Amelia said. "Jasmine can help."

"Me?"

"It'll be fun. It's so much fun."

"I won't be here much longer." As she said the words, Jasmine glanced out the window at the relentless snow.

It had to let up soon. And then she'd be free. Party or no

party. Sam or no Sam. Soon, none of it would make any difference to her in the long-term. The knowledge was vaguely depressing.

"Please, Grandma." Sophie looked so pathetically hopeful that Jasmine couldn't imagine how Belle would be able to say no.

Instead of answering, Belle spoke to Jasmine. "He went over to the house again this morning."

Jasmine was surprised. "He did?"

"He says he's going to finish the renovations, so they can move back home."

"A long time ago, Daddy tore down the dining room wall," Amelia said.

"This is a good sign?" Jasmine asked Belle.

It had to be a good sign. His trip there last night had definitely broken the ice on his emotions. Maybe the party wasn't such a bad idea after all.

"Mommy loved the party," Sophie said.

Jasmine couldn't imagine Sophie would be sophisticated enough to purposely invoke that level of emotional blackmail. But it worked anyway. Belle's shoulders drooped and her expression softened.

"Kara did love the party," Belle said to Jasmine. "And it does belong to the whole town. Last year, it was impossible, the first Christmas after. But I can't see cancelling forever. We have to start again sometime. If Sam absolutely refuses to participate, he can always stay home."

"You want to ask him up front?" Jasmine thought that might be the safer course of action.

But Belle shook her head. "No. The girls are right about that. He'll dig in his heels. It's better as a surprise."

Both of the girls shrieked with excitement.

Jasmine had some serious reservations. But this wasn't her decision to make. Kara had been Belle's daughter. Belle knew the town. And Belle obviously knew Sam better than Jasmine ever would.

"You'll help us?" Amelia asked Jasmine.

"You have to help us," Sophie said.

"I will as long as I'm here," Jasmine agreed.

She doubted she'd have time to do much, but she'd lend a hand if she could.

SAM STOOD IN his dining room, sizing up the bare studs left between it and the kitchen. He felt stronger today than he had in months. He knew with a certainty it was time to retake control of his life.

At one point in his grief, he'd decided renovating the house was the way to help them move forward. And he wasn't yet ready to throw away the idea of a fresh start. The kitchen had always been too small, and there was room in the yard to extend the living room and put in a new dining room.

His plan would mean tearing out a section of counter

and rerouting the plumbing. But he could do that. In fact, he should tear out all the counters while he was at it, and the cupboards, too.

Maybe he'd go for a lighter wood finish, or maybe even white. He liked Belle's white kitchen, it was bright and airy, fresh feeling and welcoming. Perhaps he'd also add a breakfast nook out the back. He could put in a bay window beside the vine maples, and the view would be pretty all year round.

A knock sounded on the front door, interrupting his mental sketch. His first thought was Brock, since he would have seen Sam's truck in the driveway, and he'd definitely be curious. But he quickly realized Brock would be on shift at the fire hall. Melanie then, since she would be home with the kids.

But when he pulled open the door, he was surprised to find Jasmine on his porch.

"Hi," she said simply, offering no explanation for her presence.

"What are you doing here?" He wasn't unhappy to see her, but he was definitely surprised that she would turn up.

"Belle told me you came here instead of going to work today."

"Did you walk over again?"

It looked as if she had. Her cheeks were flushed, and a fringe of her blonde hair had escaped from her hat and was damp around her face. She looked pretty. He was coming to realize she looked pretty in any outfit and any circumstance.

"It's not that far," she answered breezily.

"The snow's pretty deep."

He didn't know why he was making such a big deal. He also didn't know why he was gaping like an idiot instead of inviting her in out of the cold.

"And getting deeper." She shook off her knit hat and brushed her coat sleeves.

He stepped back out of her way. "Forgive me. Come in. You must be cold."

"Thank you." She entered the foyer and he closed the door behind her.

"So"—she glanced around the house, as if checking for details—"you came back."

"I did." He had to admit, he was still feeling good about that. He could walk into his house now like a normal person.

"Belle said you were renovating?"

"I am. I've had it in mind for a long time." He took a beat. "But, well, it got sidetracked."

Her gaze softened to moss. "You don't have to explain."

He felt himself pulled into her soothing brand of sympathy. "I get the feeling you already understand."

"I'm trying."

He was happy to have her here, happy to share his ideas with someone. The lightness and enthusiasm he was feeling was unfamiliar. It felt good, and he wasn't going to fight it.

"You want to take a look?"

"I'd like that." She removed her coat.

While he hung it in the closet, she started on her boots.

"You should keep those on." He cautioned.

"They're covered in snow."

"The house is rapidly becoming a construction zone. Don't worry about the carpets. I'll probably rip them out anyway."

"This sounds like a serious undertaking."

"I'm going big. Come on." He canted his head to the dining room before starting back.

She followed.

He quickly realized the only impressive part of the renovations were inside his head. Right now, all there was to look at was a wall of bare studs that showed through to the kitchen.

"You have to start somewhere," he said.

"You want some help?"

He couldn't help a small smile at the offer. "You know something about construction, do you?"

"Not a thing. I probably won't be all that useful."

"But you're worried about leaving me here alone?"

He'd rather ignore what had happened in the bedroom yesterday. He wasn't particularly proud of what he'd revealed. But he had to stop shying away from his emotions. The only way to get through them was to acknowledge them, assess them, and eliminate them.

"I am," she said simply.

"Don't be. What happened yesterday was the old me.

I'm better. I may still be a ways from ideal. But I'm not going to crack."

"I didn't think you were going to crack."

"That's encouraging to hear." He was tired of people tip-toeing around him.

"I want to help."

He gave her a skeptical look.

"Okay, mostly I planned to keep you company. But I can probably do something useful." She reached for a level that had been left on the table. "What is this for?"

Her earnestness made him smile. She was obviously not going to be his most able assistant. But, he'd take the company. And of all the company he could have, she would be his first choice.

"Why don't we start with the measuring tape?" He took the tape from his belt and freed up the end. "You stand there." He pointed her to one end of the counter. "Hold it steady." He positioned the tape in the right place. "Don't let it slide through your fingers. The edges aren't particularly sharp, but they can cut you if it moves too fast."

He couldn't help noticing her soft hands, the pale, ten-der skin. She definitely wasn't used to manual labor. He'd have to be careful she didn't get hurt.

"Tell me about your plans," she said, as he stretched out the tape.

"I'm going to take down this wall. But I guess that much is obvious. I'm also going to rip out the counters and cabinets. I'll have to pick something new."

The statement gave him an idea. He'd put Jasmine in charge of decorating ideas. That would be safe enough.

"I'm going to extend the living room over there." He pointed. "And add a new dining room. And I think the girls would like a breakfast nook, maybe beside the telephone counter."

She looked concerned. "That's a lot to take on."

"It's what I do."

She looked unconvinced.

"You don't like it?" he asked.

"It seems... Sudden. Are you sure you want to take on so much all at once?"

He couldn't help but feel disappointed in her reaction. "It's not so much. And it's not all of a sudden."

Now she looked contrite. "I didn't mean to imply—"

"That I'm not capable of thinking straight?"

She let go of the measuring tape, and it instantly recoiled, snapping into the receptacle in his hand.

Her shock was obvious, and she rushed forward. "Did I hurt you? Did you cut your hand?"

"You didn't hurt me." Not physically anyway. It would take a lot more than a tape measure to do that.

Her green eyes clouded, regret clear in her expression. "I didn't mean to question your judgment."

"Yet, you did."

It was baffling why he cared so much about what she

thought. She was a stranger, and her opinion didn't matter one way or the other.

"You're right. I did. And it's none of my business. It's good that you're pushing yourself. It's good that you're here with a plan for the future. It's good that you're thinking about Amelia and Sophie."

"I always think about Amelia and Sophie."

"Don't twist my words. I meant the breakfast nook."

Her defiant glare was much too close. His memory turned to their touch beside the Christmas tree.

He desperately wanted to do it again. He could feel her pressed against him. He remembered the feeling of calm that had come over him. He remembered the trickle of desire awakening inside him.

She was indescribably beautiful. Her skin was porcelain fine, her eyes big and crystal clear, her lashes dark, her nose perfectly straight and exactly the right shape. Her hair had dried, and it was a supple cloud of sunshine around her face.

His voice went gravely, lodging somewhere deep in his chest. "What are you doing to me?"

It took her a moment to answer. "I want to help."

He inched closer. "You are."

In the most unexpected way, she was reminding him that there was still life out there. She was forcing him from his shell. She was making him unpack feelings that he'd bottled up for months on end. His gaze tunneled to her full, red lips, slightly parted, unabashedly tempting.

He was going to kiss her. He was actually going to kiss her.

A knock sounded on the door, and they both startled, jumping apart.

He forced his attention away from her. "I should…"

"Yes," she agreed with a too rapid nod. "You should."

It was Melanie this time, with Libby, Grant, and Foster in tow.

"Are Amelia and Sophie here?" Libby asked eagerly.

"Not today, I'm afraid," Sam said, grateful to have the kids as a focal point so he didn't have to look Melanie in the eyes.

He felt guilty, as if he'd been caught cheating.

Libby frowned her disappointment.

"How are you, Sam?" Melanie asked.

He knew Brock had most likely shared his thoughts on Sam's state of mind, so she was probably worried about him being at the house.

"I'm good," he replied, hoping to show her exactly how well he was doing. "I'm getting started on the renovations again. Would you like to come in?"

"Sure." Something caught her attention behind him, and surprise registered on her face. "Jasmine?"

"Hi, Melanie," Jasmine responded.

"You two have met?" Sam asked as the kids trundled into the foyer.

"Yesterday," Jasmine said, coming alongside him. "While

I was picking up the decorations."

"No luck leaving town?" Melanie asked as she crouched down to unbutton Foster's jacket.

The other two kids had dropped their outerwear in the foyer and trotted into the living room.

"Everything's still shut down," Jasmine said. "The snow's supposed to let up tomorrow, but the airport will likely stay closed for several more days."

"So many areas have been hit," Melanie said. "I guess Tucker isn't a huge priority."

"Not compared to Portland and Boston." Sam said.

Libby appeared. "Are Amelia and Sophie coming home?"

"Not for a while," he said. "Did you look in the kitchen?"

She shook her head.

"You'll see it's a mess. When I'm done fixing it, the girls will be able to come home with me."

"Will that be tomorrow?"

Melanie brushed her hand over Libby's hair. "It's a very big job, honey. It's going to take Sam a long time to finish it."

Libby tipped her head to look at her mother. "Then can they come for a sleepover?"

Melanie looked to Sam with the question in her eyes.

He gave a nod of agreement. He knew the girls missed each other. It would be good for them to have some time to play.

"Sure," Melanie said.

"Goody! Let's go get them right now!"

Melanie smiled. "I don't think Sam can drop everything just because you've made some plans."

"How about this afternoon?" Sam offered. "I'll pick them up at lunch time."

He could take Jasmine back to Belle's house as well. He was torn on that. He liked having her with him, but it wasn't necessary. And he couldn't impose on her the whole day.

As SHE'D DONE every few hours for the past four days, Jasmine lifted the telephone receiver in Belle's kitchen and put it to her ear. When the dial tone buzzed, she was so shocked, she nearly dropped it.

It was back. They had communications with the outside world.

She nearly shouted to Belle who was in the living room. But she quickly stopped herself. She should make her call right away. It was nighttime in Vollan, but she didn't think the king would mind the interruption.

She pressed zero and listened to it ring a few times.

"Operator, can I help you."

"Yes, please. I'd like to place an overseas call."

"To what country, ma'am?"

"Vollan."

"Vollan?"

"Yes," Jasmine said.

"What is the number?"

"I don't know the number. It's the Royal Palace in Roxen Canal."

"I have twenty-three numbers for the Royal Palace in Roxen Canal."

"The king," Jasmine said.

"I don't have a number for the king." The operators tone turned slightly impatient.

"The main switchboard?"

"I'm putting you through."

"Wait!"

"Yes, ma'am?" This time the woman's impatience was now plainly clear.

"Can they pay the charges? The palace, I mean."

"You mean a collect call?"

"Yes." Jasmine hoped that was what she meant.

"Hold please."

Jasmine drew a breath. She took in the continued silence in the house, glad that Belle was still in the other room. There were buzzes and pings on the line, until someone finally answered.

"Vollan Royal Palace."

"I have a collect call for the king. Please state your name."

There was silence.

"Ma'am?" The operator prompted.

"Yes?" Jasmine asked.

"Please state your name."

"Oh, me. Right. It's Princess Jasmine."

Astonishment was clear in voice on the Vollan end of the call. "Your Royal Highness?"

"Will you accept the charges?" The operator repeated.

"Yes!" came the enthusiastic shout. "Yes, we will."

"Go ahead, ma'am."

There was a definitive click, and the line quality improved.

"We're so pleased to hear from you, Your Royal Highness."

"Can you put me through to my father?"

"Yes. Yes, of course. Right away."

"Thank you." Jasmine slumped back against the counter.

While she waited, she mentally composed a few opening phrases. She should assure him she was all right. She should apologize for the inconvenience. She should ask about Darren. None of this was Darren's fault. And she should make sure Costa Rhys wasn't in any trouble either.

"Jasmine?" Her father's voice was imperious as ever.

She braced herself. "Hello, Father."

"Where are you? What did you think you were *doing*?"

"I'm so sorry for the trouble."

"*Sorry*? The *trouble*? This is more than just trouble, Jasmine. Diplomats from here to Washington have been scrambling. You caused a constitutional crisis. We didn't have any idea what had happened to you. You could have been kidnapped, in danger. Your behavior was very irresponsible."

She didn't think his reaction was fair. "I sent you a message."

"We had no verification. That message could have come from anyone."

"It came from me."

His tone went hard. "You left the plane."

"I wanted some air."

"You left alone."

"It was a short walk. It was spur of the moment. Darren didn't know, and Costa didn't know."

"They've been dealt with."

"Don't fire them," she begged. "Please don't fire them."

"They've resigned."

"Get them back. I want them back." She couldn't stand that thought of ruining anyone's career.

"The jet is in Toronto. It's the closest we could get to you."

She took a few paces to the breakfast bar. It was obvious she'd have to fight for Darren and Costa's jobs once she got back home. She couldn't do it from here. "I'm fine, Father."

"We are trying for clearance into Boston." The king said. "Portland is impossible."

"You can wait until the storm's over. I can wait. I'm fine here in Tucker."

"You are completely alone. You have no security."

"I don't need security. It's a lovely little town. Everybody's friendly."

"That's hardly the way we judge threats," he said.

"There are no threats." The last thing she wanted was her father moving heaven and earth to get to her.

"A helicopter may be our only option."

"This isn't a search and rescue mission."

"Don't take that tone with me."

She re-centered herself. He was right to rebuke her for sarcasm.

"I'm trying to say that it's not an emergency, Father. I'm staying with some people—"

"What people?"

"A woman, Belle Zachary. Also with her son-in-law and his two daughters. There's nothing to worry about. They don't even know who I am."

"How do they not know who you are?" It was clear from the king's tone that he was affronted at the suggestion anyone would think she was a commoner.

She wasn't about to tell him it was fun being a commoner, that she liked being anonymous. She liked the way people treated her, the way Sam treated her, on her own merits, as if she was nobody special.

"I didn't say anything to them," she told the king. "And there's been no communication in or out of town for days. It's not like Europe. There's no reason for anyone to recognize me."

"You can't be positive they don't know."

"I am positive." Nobody had said or done a single thing that led her to believe they knew she was a princess.

"We're arranging a helicopter."

"Please don't, Father."

"We're not leaving you there any longer than necessary. You have duties. You've already missed the tree-lighting."

"I know. And I'm very sorry for that. But other people need real help." She heard a sound behind her and turned.

Sam appeared in the doorway from the laundry room. He was obviously surprised to see her on the phone. She couldn't help but wonder how much he'd overheard.

"You are not other people," said the king.

"I know." She had duties and responsibilities. Her father and many people would worry about her until she was safely home.

"We'll be there as soon as we can."

"A helicopter is not necessary."

"Yes, it is."

"Goodbye, Father."

"You need to get home." It was a command.

"I'm fine. I truly am. Please don't worry."

"Goodbye, Jasmine. I'll worry as much as I please."

"Goodbye."

The line went quiet.

She hung up the phone, and neither she nor Sam spoke.

"The phones are back," he finally stated.

"That was my father."

Sam moved into the room. "I gathered that."

"He wants me home."

"That doesn't surprise me."

"He's talking about sending a helicopter."

Sam gave a brief laugh. "I hope he owns one."

Jasmine wasn't about to admit they did own a helicopter. Although it was in Vollan not in the United States.

He moved to the refrigerator and selected a beer. Then he held it out to her as an offer. She shook her head.

"We're still in a state of emergency. Every available helicopter will be deployed in the recovery effort. I'm not sure you'd even get clearance to fly one in.

"I told him I was fine."

"I heard that."

"What else did you hear?" She figured she might as well know the truth, or at least know how much of the truth Sam now knew.

"I wasn't eavesdropping."

"I didn't think you were."

"You saw when I walked in."

"I did." And if that was all he'd heard, she was still safely incognito.

He moved toward her. "Was there something else?"

She played dumb. "What do you mean?"

"Was there something you said that you didn't want me

to hear?" There was a teasing note to his voice that put her at ease. "Something unsavory, possibly illegal."

She was relieved to play along with the joke. "What are you imagining?"

"I have to wonder…" He paused, obviously for effect. "Where did all that money come from?"

She tilted her head. "Are you accusing me of belonging to a crime family?"

"Do you belong to a crime family?"

"I do not. We are incredibly respectable."

"I'm going to take you at your word."

"How very generous of you."

It was clear he was fighting a smile. "But only because you're so adorable."

His words sent a rush of happiness through her. She knew he was joking, but the compliment warmed her to her core.

He seemed to realize what he'd said, and his expression sobered. "I mean…"

She jumped in. "You mean I have an air of innocence?"

It took him a moment to answer. "Yes, that's it."

"I'm glad." She wanted to recapture their joking mood. "I'd hate to be saddled with an air of guilt."

Chapter Six

A S HE AND Brock cut away the studs from the dining room wall, Sam couldn't stop himself from hoping that Jasmine would somehow be forced to stay longer. The snow had stopped last night, and the sun was finally out. Though the airport was still closed for the moment, he knew the clock was ticking. By all accounts, her father was extremely anxious to get her home.

Not that Sam blamed the man. It had to be unsettling to have your daughter, even an adult daughter, stranded by a storm and completely out of contact. Still, Jasmine was twenty-four-years old. Surely she could decide to spend some extra time in Maine. Sam would have her home in time for Christmas.

As he pondered Jasmine staying in Tucker to be with him, he switched the power off on his reciprocating saw and glanced at her profile. She was seated in the living room with Melanie, their heads bent over Melanie's laptop. With the internet back up, they were browsing kitchen cabinet stores and looking for decorating ideas.

"Something wrong?" Brock asked, peeling off his own

safety goggles.

"Just taking a breather," Sam said.

Brock moved closer, taking in the focus of Sam's gaze. "She's pretty."

Guilt instantly hit Sam. "It's not like that."

"It's allowed to be like that."

Sam gave his friend a frown.

"You're human, Sam. You're a thirty-year-old man with normal instincts. Whether you want to or not, you're going to notice pretty women."

"I haven't so far."

It was true. Maybe it was because he knew almost every twenty or thirty something woman in Tucker. Or maybe it was because his emotions had been shut down for so long. But he hadn't noticed any pretty women till now, and he certainly hadn't been attracted to anyone.

"Then this is a good sign."

"This is nothing," Sam said. He wasn't ready for it to be something.

"You keep watching her."

"I'm curious about her." That much was true. "Belle and the kids think she's great. And she seems to like it here. But she's got this overbearing father back in Vollan who seems almost panicked about getting her home. He was talking about sending in a chopper."

"To rescue her from Tucker?"

"Isn't that nuts? Sure, there's been a storm, but it's not

exactly a disaster area."

"The town's still putting up Christmas decorations," Brock said.

"Most festive disaster area I've ever seen."

Brock chuckled.

"I keep picturing a SWAT team showing up at Belle's house and hustling Jasmine away in the dead of night."

"And how does that make you feel?"

Sam opened his mouth to answer, but then he realized Brock had set a trap. "Surprised," he said.

"Not disappointed? Not sad? Not lonely?"

"You're making this into something it's not."

"I guess I'm just hoping."

"That I'll replace Kara?"

"No." Brock put his hand on Sam's shoulder. "You'll never replace Kara."

"I know I won't." Sam would love her until the day he died.

"I'm just happy to see you feeling better. I'm thrilled to help you finish the kitchen."

Sam knew Brock was being a good friend. And he appreciated it more than Brock could know.

He took in their progress for the day. "It's looking good. I was thinking after we're done, I should look at replacing the carpets in living room."

"As soon as Foster starts school, we're replacing ours. Toddlers are hard on floors."

"Amelia and Sophie are definitely neater than they used to be. Now, that could be Belle's influence."

"They're also girls. Count yourself lucky that you didn't have boys."

"I was once a boy. I remember."

Brock grinned again, moving back to the opposite end of the half-demolished wall where he was coiling the electrical wires. "You know how these things go. You'll replace the carpet, then decide to paint the walls, then decide the stairs needs work, and pretty soon you'll be upstairs sizing up the bedrooms."

"I may add an en suite bathroom to the master. Now that the girls are getting older, privacy is going to be important."

"I've always thought you should punch out the wall to that sitting room. It seems to be dead storage space, and you'd end up with a fantastic master."

Sam pictured it in his mind. It was a good idea. It was the wall he'd put his fist through, and removing it altogether appealed to him.

"You know you're signing up for a whole lot of neighborly work." He warned Brock.

"It's not like you can do the exterior walls before spring. We might as well do something in the meantime."

"We might as well."

A month ago, Sam would have been overwhelmed by such an enormous task. But now it seemed to energize him.

Melanie called from the living room. "What do you think of beechwood cabinets?"

"I'm open," Sam said. As long as it was fresh and light, he wasn't going to fuss about the details.

Jasmine came to her feet, moving gracefully across the room. "Something like this? The natural wood would soften the light." She came up close beside him and showed him the laptop. "You could do pale yellow on the walls, mottled green countertops, and add some stone accents."

He loved the sound of her voice. He loved the scent of her skin. He liked having her close. Her arm touched his and he subtly leaned in, making a show of adjusting the screen of the laptop so he could see it clearly.

It wasn't the only thing he could see.

He'd just denied it up and down to Brock. But he was lying, and he'd been lying to himself for days. He was intensely attracted to Jasmine—a man to a woman, romantically and sexually, in every way possible. It might be too soon, but it was what it was, and there was no way to stop it.

"I like that," he said about the picture.

"It sounds expensive," Brock said.

Jasmine's expression fell, and Sam's instinct was to defend her choice. "I don't mind paying for good quality."

"I didn't think about the cost." She looked quite regretful.

"Don't worry about it," he said. "Show me what you're thinking."

She seemed to be gauging the sincerity in his expression.

"Go ahead." He prompted.

"Okay." She turned her attention to the screen, pointing. "It would be bright without being glaring, up-to-date, but timeless enough to endure trends, making it worth the money in the long run."

"Don't worry about money this early on."

She gave him a grateful smile. "I was thinking this corner shelf would look great with small plants, succulents, low maintenance, maybe in jade colored pots."

"Sounds good to me." Quite frankly, he was ready to agree to anything she proposed.

"Are you guys getting hungry?" Melanie asked.

"I'm hungry," Brock said.

"Jasmine and I can go make some sandwiches."

Sam was hungry, too. But he didn't want Jasmine to go make sandwiches. He didn't want her to go anywhere. He wanted her to stay right here beside him where he could touch her and smell her.

He wanted desperately to kiss her, and he was tired of fighting his desire. It suddenly seemed like every facet of his life was a battle. He wanted to let go now. He wanted to take the easy path, the pleasant path. Would it be so terrible if he was to kiss Jasmine?

"The babysitter needs to head home soon," Melanie said. "Jasmine can bring the food back. That is, unless you want five children underfoot while you work."

"Please, spare us," Brock said. "The boys love to 'help'."

Sam knew it was inefficient, but he couldn't help but smile at the image. But then his smile faded as Jasmine walked away from him. She left the laptop on the table and bundled into her coat and hat.

As the door closed behind the women, Brock spoke. "Good thing you're not attracted to her."

"I'd have to be blind not to notice she's attractive."

"Well, that's progress. At least you're not falling all over yourself to pretend you're made of stone."

"I'm not made of stone."

"None of us are made of stone. Let your guard down. Let yourself go. I promise the world will continue to spin."

"What can I do? She's here for a couple more days, at most." Continuing to lie to Brock seemed pointless at this stage.

"There's another storm coming in."

"Yeah?" Hope rose in Sam.

Brock chuckled. "You've got it bad."

"You're wrong. I've got it. Sure. But just barely."

Sam was attracted to Jasmine, full stop. She was a beautiful, kind, and intelligent woman. The attraction was perfectly understandable and perfectly ordinary, and it would fade to a fuzzy memory by New Year's.

AMELIA, SOPHIE, AND Libby shrieked with delight, playing

some kind of chasing game up and down the staircase in Melanie's house.

Melanie covered her ears. "One minute it's dress-up and dolls, the next it's tag."

Grant rushed by, followed by Foster, bringing up the rear.

"Is that why Foster's wearing lipstick?" Jasmine asked.

"Grant's starting to refuse, but Foster's still up for anything."

"Amelia and Sophie showed me their dress-up clothes."

They were sitting at Melanie's dining room table sharing tea.

"They have the best collection in town," Melanie said. "Some came from Kara, but most from Belle. I think Belle still collects them from used clothing stores when she travels. She was quite the fashionista when she was young."

"But not Kara?" Jasmine asked. She couldn't help but be curious about Kara, but she didn't want to ask her family about her. It could too easily bring back painful memories.

"Kara was more of a tomboy," Melanie said. "I think that's what first attracted Sam. She was the only girl willing to help him build a tree fort."

"You grew up with them, then?"

"We were all in the same school, Brock, me, Sam, and Kara. You must wonder about her."

"I haven't wanted to ask."

"She was great, loads of fun, up for anything, athletic,

good at yard work."

Jasmine couldn't help contrasting herself to Kara. She wasn't athletic. And doubted she'd be any good at yard work. She wasn't even sure exactly what yard work would be.

Was she fun? Fun was probably not the right word. She liked to think she was kind and supportive. She could host a great event. Then again, anybody could host a great event with a staff of fifty. She'd never actually tried it on her own.

She knew four languages. But she doubted that was much fun for children. For the first time, she wondered about being a mother. Would her children like her? Royal mothers didn't have time for a lot of play.

Melanie continued speaking. "I'd say Kara was a perfect mother for Amelia. Sophie is more like her grandmother. So it's nice having Belle around."

"They said Kara played dress-up with them."

"She did. So did I. I think we moms feign enthusiasm for a whole lot of things. Dress-up is a staple for young girls here in Tucker. What about you?"

Jasmine wasn't sure how to answer. She didn't want to admit she was worried about her mothering capabilities.

"Did you play dress-up?" Melanie elaborated.

Jasmine laughed at that, relieved that the question was more straightforward than her eventual plans for mother-hood. "No. I had to do dress-up for real."

"How so?"

Jasmine had been a feature at balls and afternoon teas

from the time she was four years old. No expense had been spared designing gowns and accessories for the little princess. But she couldn't tell that to Melanie.

"Sam may have mentioned, in Vollan, my father has a fair amount of influence and, well, money, too."

"You grew up rich?"

"I guess there's really no other word for it. I'm an only child, and there were a lot of formal events while I was growing up."

"Dress-up isn't as much fun in real life?" Melanie guessed.

"It loses something when you have to stand and smile for hours."

The children flashed past again, in a blur of color and noise. They were obviously running some kind of circuit through the house. Melanie seemed to take it all in stride.

"Tell me more about Kara," Jasmine prompted. "If you don't mind, that is."

"I don't mind. I like talking about her. She was something of a leader in the PTA and in the neighborhood. She fund-raised for school field trips, went on the field trips, organized the soccer league, and led the street beautification project. Flowers she planted still bloom."

"That's a nice legacy." Jasmine had planted countless trees around Vollan. She liked to think about them still standing, bringing beauty and shade to the parks and memorials.

"We were close for the years they lived here," Melanie said.

"You must miss her."

"I do. But, well, it's starting to feel like a long time has gone past. The memories are good, but so much has changed now, with the girls growing up. Foster was just a baby back then. A lot about my life has changed."

"Mommy?" It was Libby who spoke, but the other children all arrived around her in a cluster.

"The busyness factor hasn't changed," Melanie said with a good natured laugh. "Yes, honey?"

"How are we going to make our costumes? For the Christmas party. How are we going to make the costumes on time?"

"Costumes," Foster sang. "Costumes."

Melanie took a moment to answer, obviously composing her words. "We might not have time for costumes this year."

The girls' faces fell.

Sophie swallowed.

"We have to have costumes," Amelia whispered in what seemed like horror.

"What kind of costumes do you need?" Jasmine asked.

"We did elves last time," Libby said. "All the kids in school were elves."

"And once we did angels," Amelia said.

"Santa toys one year," Melanie said. "But they took weeks to make. Even with everyone pitching in, there's already so much to do in a short time."

A large tear appeared in the corner of Sophie's eye.

Amelia took her hand.

Libby compressed her lips.

"What about your dress-up clothes," Jasmine suggested.

Five sets of eyes swung her way. Melanie looked curious as well.

"You have all those wonderful dresses and things in your basement. I bet your friends have some, too. Maybe you could use them and be Christmas princesses?" She looked to Grant. "And Christmas princes, too, of course."

The girls broke into instantaneous smiles. "*Christmas princesses*," they cried.

"Can we, Mommy," Libby asked, jumping on the spot. "Can we?"

"That sounds easy enough," said Melanie. She reached out to give Jasmine's hand a squeeze. "Let me talk to Belle and some of the other mommies."

"Let's go downstairs and look," called Amelia, turning to trot away.

"We can all share," said Libby. "We can trade."

It took Foster a minute to realize the group was moving on, but then he gamely trotted after them.

"Nice save," Melanie said.

"You obviously know about the party plan."

"With the phones up and running, Belle's been organizing us into squads."

"What do you think?"

"Of surprising Sam?"

Jasmine nodded, while Melanie took a contemplative sip of her tea.

"It's a risk," Melanie said. "But seeing him today, I think it's a risk worth taking."

"Belle said the same thing."

"You didn't see what he was like. As late as a week ago, he wasn't going near his house, and he was determined to endure the holidays in abject misery. Brock was at the end of his rope, about to force the issue one way or the other."

"These last couple of days..." Jasmine began. Even she had noticed a change in the short time she'd known him.

"Brock thinks it's you."

Jasmine stilled in surprise. "How could it be me?"

"You've shaken him up. He sees you as a woman."

"I am a woman."

"He's attracted to you."

"Nothing's happened," Jasmine hastily assured her. The last thing she wanted was for Sam to be the subject of gossip on top of everything else.

"I'm not surprised by that. He's fighting it for all he's worth. But he's also turned a corner. You're good for him. He needs you."

Jasmine knew that couldn't be true. "He barely knows me."

"It doesn't matter."

"I'm only going to be here a few more days."

"A few days is a long time," Melanie said with a sly smile.

Jasmine wasn't going there. The very thought of something happening between them—even if Jasmine had privately fantasized in the dead of night—was absolutely out of the question. Sam was a recovering widower and Jasmine was a princess. She had a code of conduct to respect, and duties that she was already neglecting on the other side of the ocean. Kissing Sam might be a compelling daydream, but that was all it could ever be.

"It's a bad idea," Jasmine said. "It's a really bad idea."

"But you're tempted."

Jasmine felt her cheeks heat and she focused on her tea.

"I saw the way you looked at him," Melanie said.

"He's a nice-looking man." Jasmine's words were an almost comical understatement.

"You don't have to be embarrassed."

"I'm not embarrassed."

"You're blushing. You're an adult. You're single. There's nothing wrong with being attracted to Sam."

Melanie didn't understand the complexities. Jasmine might be an adult, but she was completely innocent where it came to romance. Casual dating wasn't a constitutionally permitted activity for the crown princess. Even if it was, she doubted any man in Vollan would brave her father in order to date her.

"Shake him up a little," Melanie said. "Rattle his cage."

"I'm not rattling anything when it comes to Sam. I'm leaving everything"—Jasmine held up her palms for emphasis—"completely un-rattled."

Melanie laughed. "It's your decision. But if the moment presents itself, I say you should go for it."

Jasmine's cheeks grew warmer still. The last thing she wanted was a moment with Sam to present itself. Because she might not be able to stop herself from going for it, and that would be a disaster.

She took a swallow of tea and tried to keep her imagination from wandering.

It would be an utterly exciting, indulgent, exhilarating disaster.

AT THE END of the day, Sam was dusty and tired, but satisfied. They'd made significant progress dismantling the kitchen, and started planning the new layout. Brock went home to his family, while Sam and Jasmine settled in the pickup truck for the short drive to Belle's.

He adjusted the fan speed to keep cold air from blowing on them while the engine warmed up. "Do you mind if we take a detour?"

"Not at all." She wrapped her arms around herself.

"Cold?"

"A little. But I'll be fine. Where are we going?"

"Walnut Crescent." He pulled forward and turned onto

the street. "There's a seniors' residence a few blocks in. I've been trying to plow a street or two on my way home every night."

"That's very considerate of you." It was dark in the cab, but he could hear a smile in her voice.

"A few of us have plow blades on our trucks. It's mostly felt like a losing battle, but every little bit we can clear makes it easier for people to get around."

"You've very civic-minded."

"I was. I used to be, before—" He caught himself, not wanting to risk getting emotional. He'd been strong all day and he was determined to stay that way.

"It sounds like you still are," Jasmine said.

"I'm getting there."

It felt good to be thinking about other people. Maybe that was what he should have been doing all along. Maybe he'd been too self-indulgent about his own sorrow. He should have snapped out of this months ago.

"There's no right way to grieve," Jasmine said, her voice sympathetic in the dim light of the cab.

"I'm beginning to think there's a wrong way."

"There's only your way. Melanie thinks you're feeling better."

He didn't know how to respond to the opening. He'd been guarding himself for so long, it was almost impossible to let go and be honest. But he found he wanted to be honest. He wanted to open up to Jasmine.

She waited quietly.

"It's strange," he finally said as he navigated the snowy street. "It's like I stepped out of a bubble. Suddenly, I can hear, smell, touch, and taste things I'd almost forgotten existed."

Walnut Crescent was coming up.

"Two weeks ago, I'd have told you it was impossible for me to pack Kara's clothes into a box."

"You packed up her clothes?"

"This morning." He signaled, turned left onto Walnut, and lowered the plow blade.

The truck lurched with the increased load, and Jasmine grabbed for the dashboard to brace herself.

"You okay?" he asked.

"Fine."

"It's going to be bumpy." He should have thought of that before he decided on this plan.

"I'm good."

He considered taking advantage of the interruption and letting the subject of Kara's clothes drop. But he found he didn't want to do that. Strangely, he wanted to talk about his reactions to being in the house.

"I put her stuff in the basement," he said, adjusting the speed of the truck, gauging the resistance of the snow. "I'm going to renovate the master bedroom." No, that wasn't what he wanted to say. He could talk to Brock and Melanie about the physical aspects of the house. He wanted, needed to talk to someone about the emotional impact of the changes he was making.

"It's hard," he said to Jasmine, forcing himself to lay out the truth. "Part of me wants to hide it all away, replace the furniture, rip out the carpets. And part of me wants to freeze it all in time." He paused. "But I suppose that's what I've been doing. And it hasn't been working. I need to change something. I need to move forward. But it scares me half to death."

He realized just how much he'd said and he snapped his jaw shut, using the excuse of backing up the truck to relieve the load on the plow, in order to get himself out of the intensely personal conversation.

"I think it used to scare you," Jasmine said. "I think it stopped scaring you, and that's what's scaring you."

He put the truck into drive again. But he kept his foot on the brake pedal, turning to look at her. A streetlight shone through the window, highlighting her blond hair, framing her beautiful face, her green eyes opaque and compassionate.

She was right.

The frightening part was that he *could* let go.

"Who are you?" he asked.

She suddenly seemed to tense up. "What do you mean?"

"I mean how did you come into my life?"

As quickly as she'd gone tense, she seemed to relax again. "There was a plane, and a storm, and your mother-in-law."

He couldn't help but smile at her joke. "To think I've been cursing this storm."

"*I've* certainly been cursing this storm." She stopped. "I'm sorry. I didn't mean that that way it sounded. I'm happy I met you, Sam."

The desire that rose up in him was so strong, that he all but bent the steering wheel under his grip. He forced himself to look away from her, forced himself to lift his foot from the brake, touching the accelerator and sending the truck forward.

"Sam, look out!" she cried.

He hit the brakes again, sliding to a halt, stopping just short of a mottled brown dog that looked trapped in the snow. It was medium sized, with short hair, and floppy ears. It stared up at the truck with such a sad and desperate look that Sam was immediately out the door, clambering through the snow towards it.

"Hey, boy," he said gently, offering the back of his hand for it to sniff.

The dog whimpered. It tried to move in the deep snow, but it was obviously too exhausted.

He heard Jasmine's door open. "Do you need help?"

"Stay put," he called back. "The snow is really deep."

"Are you lost?" he asked the dog.

He checked for a collar, but didn't find one.

The dog was shivering.

Sam stroked its fur. "Would you come with me?" he

asked in the most soothing voice he could muster.

Careful not to startle the animal, he slid one arm across its chest and one behind its haunches.

"Try to keep still," he said, slowly lifting the dog, coming fully to his feet.

Though he followed his own footsteps back, it was still a struggle. But he made it to the truck, and hoisted the dog onto the bench seat in the cab.

"It he okay?" Jasmine asked in a hushed voice.

"Exhausted," Sam said. "Really cold. He must be hungry and thirsty."

She scratched the dog under its chin. It immediately flopped down in the middle of the seat and put its head in her lap.

She glanced around the neighborhood. "Should we check the houses?"

"Maybe tomorrow," Sam answered. It would take a long time to wade his way up to each house, and he had to assume if someone close by was missing a dog, they'd have come looking for it.

"You'll take him home?" Jasmine asked. Her tone said she was afraid he might say no.

"Absolutely," Sam said. "Belle might not love it on her white floor, but we can't leave him out here."

"Good." She sounded relieved.

The dog closed its eyes and its shivering stopped. Its breathing went even.

"He's obviously used to people," Sam said.

"He seems thin."

Sam thought so, too. He had to wonder how long the dog had been away from its home. If it was for the entirety of the storm, it was a good thing they'd found him when they did.

"It won't take long to finish the plowing," Sam said.

"He seems comfortable," Jasmine said.

"You don't mind him there."

"I don't mind at all. I've always wanted a dog." She gently stroked his fur. "My father's a cat person." A smile came onto her face. "Fiona and Mitander. Both pure white Persians."

"I bet they have jeweled collars."

"You'd bet right. Fiona's is ruby and Mitander's is emerald."

"Not real ones."

Jasmine gave a little laugh. "No, no, not real."

But there was something in the way she said it that made him wonder just exactly how rich her family was.

"What about yours?" he asked.

"My dog? I just said I didn't have one."

"I meant your jewelry. Is it all real?"

She hesitated a moment before answering. "Some. It's mostly heirlooms. I don't buy much myself."

"Daddy doesn't buy it for you?"

"Was that an insult?"

Sam realized he had been rude. "I apologize. What your father does or doesn't buy you is none of my business."

"I'm not spoiled, Sam. I mean, well, I know that I *am* privileged."

"You have a private jet." He reversed the truck again, freeing it from the large pile of snow that had built up in front of the plow blade. He changed the angle.

"My family has a private jet. I was only using it."

He couldn't stop a smirk. "You do know how that sounded."

"*Yes*, I *know* how that sounded. But I can't help who I was born."

"Did I touch a nerve?"

"No. It is what it is." She sounded more resigned than content.

That made him curious. "Would you change it if you could?"

The question obviously made her think, and he got the sense she was planning on giving him a straight answer rather than a flippant one. He admired that.

"Mostly, no," she said. "But every once in a while, in a moment like this, I think it would be nice to be someone else, someone normal."

The intimacy of the cab seemed to press in around them, and he couldn't stop himself from asking. "What do you like about this moment?"

She kept her gaze down, concentrating on the dog. "The

night. The stillness. The privacy." Her voice softened. "The company."

Emotion swelled inside him. He didn't say anything. But he stretched his arm to touch her shoulder. He stroked it with his fingertips.

She covered his hand with hers, and he reveled in the pleasant feelings that flowed from the touch.

"There's something going on here, isn't there?" he asked.

She opened her mouth, then closed it again, waiting a moment before she spoke. "There can't be."

He supposed that was true, but he knew now it wasn't something they could will away. He wanted her. And she had as much as admitted she was attracted right back.

"It's a good thing there's a dog between us." He punched through the snow at the end of the crescent, back out to the main road.

Chapter Seven

"WE GOT A dog!" Amelia cried out as she entered the kitchen and spotted the animal standing next to Sam.

Belle appeared, looking next to horrified by the scene. "What's this?"

Jasmine was impressed the dog stayed calm through the commotion.

"He's just visiting," Sam cautioned Amelia, obviously also intending to reassure Belle.

Sophie came sliding around the corner, her sock feet scrambling against the slippery floor before she grabbed onto Belle for stability. "We got a *dog?*"

"We found him stuck in the snow." Sam explained to Belle.

"You better start looking for his owner," Belle said without missing a beat.

It was easy to see she wasn't a dog lover.

"What's his name?" Amelia asked.

"We don't know," Sam said. "We'll look for his owner tomorrow."

"Can't we keep him?" Sophie asked.

"No, we can't keep him," Belle immediately answered.

"For now, he's hungry," Sam said. "There are some left-over burgers."

"Why can't we keep him?" asked Sophie.

"Is he friendly?" asked Amelia, inching closer.

"He seems friendly," Jasmine said. "He slept with his head in my lap on the way home."

"We have to name him," Amelia said. She approached the dog, holding out her hand to let him sniff it, just as Sam had done back on the road.

The dog gave her a sniff then a lick.

"He likes me!"

"Or he's hungry," Belle harrumphed.

Jasmine found herself sharing a smile with Sam.

"I found him a bowl," Sophie announced, proudly holding up a red ceramic bowl.

"Not my good mixing bowl," Belle said.

"Get one of the empty ice cream tubs from the laundry room," Sam said.

"I'll get it," Amelia announced from where she was closer to the door.

"Me, too," Sophie echoed, dashing after her sister.

"I'm not having a strange dog running all over my house," Belle said.

"It's just overnight," Sam said. "And I won't let him run loose."

"How do we know he's not dangerous?"

"I won't leave him unsupervised with the girls. And he can come to work with me in the morning."

"I can smell him from here."

Jasmine had noticed in the truck, that the dog was somewhat aromatic.

"He'll need a bath before he sleeps in this house," Belle said.

Sam seemed taken aback by the suggestion.

"I can help," Jasmine quickly offered.

"Use the steel tub in the garage," Belle said. "I want you to keep the mess outside the house."

"We got an ice cream tub," Sophie announced, re-entering the room.

Amelia held the plastic tub in her hands and looked around the kitchen for a place to put it down.

"Beside the fridge." Belle directed, seeming to have given into the inevitable. "Take the hamburger patties out of the green container. Make sure you break them into small pieces."

Amelia placed the makeshift dog dish, while Sophie opened the fridge, hunting through it.

"Found it," she called.

Jasmine was enjoying the girls' excitement. At that age, she would have been over the moon to have a dog in the palace. She could imagine she'd have behaved exactly the same way.

The dog stayed close to Sam, pressing against his leg while the girls ran around. Even when the burgers appeared, and the girls broke them up and dropped them in the dish, the dog stayed put.

Finished, they stood back and waited expectantly.

Sam looked down. "Come on then," he said to the dog.

He walked to the dish and the dog went with him. But it wasn't until he pointed to the dish and said "it's yours," that the dog began to eat.

"He's well-trained," Jasmine said.

"Very well-trained," Sam said. "He'll need some water, too, girls."

They immediately scrambled back to the laundry room.

"I'll make some phone calls tomorrow," Sam said to Belle.

"Maybe," she responded.

He gave her a questioning look.

Jasmine couldn't believe Belle had changed her mind that quickly. Had the dog won her over?

"Another big storm is rolling in," Belle said. "We might lose phone service again."

"Another one?" Jasmine couldn't believe it might happen all over again.

"That's the prediction."

"We'll figure it out," Sam said.

Jasmine assumed he was talking about the dog. But she looked up and realized he was talking to her.

"We'll get you home," he told her gently.

"It has to happen eventually," she said.

She was less upset than she should have been at another potential delay. And gazing at Sam, she knew the reason why. She could still feel his hand on her shoulder, still hear his evocative words. It might be wrong, and it might be impossible, but she wasn't ready to leave him. She couldn't muster up any enthusiasm for getting back home.

The girls returned with a second plastic tub and headed for the sink to fill it.

"We have to name him," Amelia said.

"We can't just call him dog," Sophie said.

"He doesn't have a collar," Sam said. "I checked."

"What about Spot?" Amelia asked.

"He doesn't really have spots."

"Mr. Snowman," Sophie said. "Because you found him in the snow."

"That's silly," Amelia said.

"It's a mouthful," Jasmine said, gazing at the dog, trying to come up with something that suited him.

"Rover?" Belle asked.

Sam gave her a look. "Really?"

She shrugged. "It's tried and true."

"Mr. Storm," Sophie said. "Because you found him in a storm."

"Storm," Jasmine tried out.

"Hey, Storm," Sam called.

The dog looked up. He gave one short bark then went back to eating.

"Storm it is," Sam said.

"Storm, Storm," the girls chorused.

"Let him eat."

They sobered. "Yes, Daddy."

Sophie leaned against her sister. "We've got a dog," she whispered, cheeks glowing and eyes shining.

"Only for tonight," Amelia whispered back.

"We might not find his owner."

Amelia broke into a grin at the prospect.

Belle raised her eyebrows at Sam, a clear "now look what you've done" expression on her face. She shook her head and left the kitchen.

"I think I'm in trouble," Sam whispered to Jasmine.

She nodded to the girls. "You're their hero."

Their attention was rapt on Storm.

"Were you serious about helping with the bath?" Sam asked her.

"I've never done it before. But I'm willing to try."

She'd add it to the list of new things she'd tried since landing in Tucker. With some, like flipping pancakes, she been successful. With others, not so much. But they were all interesting. And bathing the dog would keep her with Sam. Right now, she wanted to be with Sam.

Storm finished his meal, and the girls made a fuss over him for a while, while Sam and Jasmine sat at the breakfast bar and watched.

"Have you eaten dinner?" He asked his daughters.

"We had chicken pie," said Amelia.

"Then it's time for pajamas."

"Aww. Do we have to?"

"We want to play with Storm."

"We're not tired."

"You can play with him again in the morning. He's going for a bath now." Sam looked to Jasmine. "Okay with you if we eat after the bath."

"That's fine with me." She was hungry, but she could wait. She'd rather get the work done and get cleaned up first.

Sam came to his feet. "Come on, Storm."

Storm immediately obeyed.

"You could learn a thing or two from him," Sam told his daughters.

"Yes, Daddy." They both gave an exaggerated sigh.

"Come and give me a kiss."

Having accepted their fate, the two girls happily kissed Sam goodnight. Then, to Jasmine's surprise, they each gave her a kiss as well.

"Night, Jasmine," said Amelia.

Sophie wrapped her arms around Jasmine's neck and gave her a tight squeeze. "See you in the morning."

"Goodnight, sweeties," Jasmine managed as her throat clogged with emotion. "Sleep well."

"Ever done this before?" Sam asked her as the girls reluctantly left the room.

"This will be a first," she said, sizing up Storm who looked relaxed and happy after eating.

This would definitely be a first for her. As a child, she'd occasionally watched the stable grooms lather and hose down the horses. It hadn't looked that hard, a little messy, maybe. But the horses hadn't seemed to mind the process.

"Me neither." Sam seemed to be sizing up the dog as well.

"There's some shampoo in my bathroom," she offered.

"You want him to smell like lavender?"

Jasmine was surprised Sam knew what her shampoo smelled like. Then she was pleased. Then she was aroused. This was not good.

Sam opened the cupboard below the kitchen sink, extracting a large bottle of blue liquid. "This seems neutral enough."

"Do you think the dog will care?"

"No male wants to smell like flowers. It's unmanly."

"Like wearing pink?"

"I'm not putting Storm in anything pink."

"I meant you." She realized as she said it that it would be impossible to tone down Sam's masculinity, no matter what color he wore.

"Pink? No. I do have a periwinkle dress shirt."

"Blue? Your idea of feminine is blue?"

"Periwinkle isn't a man's color. I only bought it to go

with one of Kara's dresses. She insisted. I thought it was silly."

Jasmine couldn't help but notice the casual way in which he talked about Kara. She couldn't help thinking that was enormous progress.

"Come on, Storm," Sam said.

The dog immediately went to him, falling into step.

"Sorry about this, buddy." Sam apologized as they headed through the laundry room.

"He might like it," Jasmine offered, hoping her words would prove true.

"He might endure it without complaint. We guys are like that."

She laughed as Sam opened the door to the garage.

He turned on the light, and they climbed down the short staircase.

Sam quickly located the old steel tub, pulled it from behind some cardboard boxes, and set it in an open spot on the concrete floor.

He then located some buckets under a laundry sink.

"Should we use warm water?" Jasmine asked, joining him there.

"It might make the experience more pleasant."

"I've watched the royal—" She quickly stopped herself.

"The what?" he prompted, positioning a bucket and twisting the taps to full.

"When I was a girl, I watched the grooms bath the horses."

"You have horses?"

"My family has horses."

"Do you ride?"

"Yes."

"I can picture you doing that."

"You?" she asked.

"Dirt bikes, not horses. When we were teenagers, Brock and I used to tear up the hills out back all summer long."

"Melanie said you grew up in Tucker."

"All my life." He hoisted the first bucket from the deep sink, setting it on the floor.

"It seems like a nice place to grow up. I mean, what I've seen of it." She realized she'd like to see it in the summertime, stroll down Main Street, meet some of the people.

"It was a great place to grow up. That's why I'm raising the girls here." He'd filled another bucket and set it down.

Storm was cruising the perimeter of the garage, sniffing his way from object to object. The air was chilled, and goose bumps had come up on Jasmine's arms. But she knew she couldn't wear a jacket for the dog bath. It would be awkward and she was bound to get wet.

"Your parents?" she asked. "Are they still living in Tucker?"

"They retired to Silent Lake. It's about two-hundred miles north, near the border. We had a cabin there for years and they upgraded it to a house."

"Will they come back for Christmas?"

"They were planning to be here. If there's another storm coming, they might not make it."

Jasmine moved to where she could see out a window toward the streetlight. Sure enough, the flakes were beginning to fall, shimmering through the pool of light, still pretty, even though it meant more chaos.

"It's starting to snow," she said.

"I guess we knew that was coming." Sam lifted two of the full buckets and moved them the short distance to the tub.

"Come here, Storm," he called, and the dog obeyed.

Jasmine fished out the hair elastic that she habitually kept on hand. Over the years, she'd learned to be prepared for unexpected wind at unexpected photo ops. Her father hated it when she appeared windblown in the newspapers.

She fastened her hair back and squared herself up to the wash tub.

At first Storm looked confused, but when Sam insisted, the dog stepped gingerly into the tub.

"I wish he had a collar," Sam said. "If I brace him, can you pour?"

"Yes."

He wrapped an arm around the dog's neck.

"I hope you're ready," Jasmine muttered as she slowly poured the tepid water over Storm's back.

The dog jolted and turned to look.

"It's okay, buddy." Sam crooned. "I know just how you

feel."

Storm tried to wiggle out of Sam's arms, but Sam held tight.

"The soap," Sam prompted. "You might want to make it fast."

Jasmine squirted some dish soap into her hands. Then she rubbed them together and applied it to Storm's back.

The dog liked that even less.

"Hurry," Sam said.

"I'm hurrying."

She rubbed around his belly, down his legs, and up his neck. All the while, he wiggled harder, panting, and straining to see what she was doing.

"I'm sorry." She apologized to him. "But you'll feel better, I promise."

"He's getting slippery," Sam warned.

"Should I rinse?"

"You better. I don't know how much longer I can—"

Storm gave a mighty lunge and broke Sam's hold. He rushed across the garage, slipping as he turned corners, shaking the foam from his body, sending it flying everywhere.

"Oh, that's not good," Sam said.

Jasmine couldn't help it. She rose to her feet and started to laugh.

Sam shot her a warning look. Then his gaze dropped and held, a hungry expression coming into his eyes.

She looked down to see her body outlined by the cling-ing wet t-shirt. She went hot, then cold, then hot all over again.

Seconds slipped by in slow motion.

Then he reached out and his hand closed over her shoul-der. He gently but firmly drew her forward.

She didn't resist, and before she had a chance to think, his lips were on hers.

They were hot and tender, malleable and mobile. The contact thrilled her to her toes. Heat rolled through her. It might be her first kiss, but her body seemed to know exactly what to do. It molded itself against him, drinking in every nuance of his muscular chest, hard abs, and strong thighs.

His arms went around her, enfolding her. She felt safer than she ever had before. She wrapped her arms around his neck, touching his hair, reveling in its texture.

He gently broke the kiss. "Jasmine." He breathed out a long, satisfied sigh. Then he touched his forehead to hers. "I didn't mean to do that."

She gave a little nod of acknowledgment.

"I haven't felt this way in a very long time," he said.

"Neither have I." She decided never could be considered a very long time.

"I don't know what to do about this." He seemed to be choosing his words carefully. "I'm not... I mean... I guess you know perfectly well where I'm at emotionally."

She drew back just far enough to look into his eyes. "I'm

not either, Sam. I'm in no position to get emotionally involved with anyone."

"I know you have to go home."

"It's more than that."

She suddenly wanted to tell him the truth, be honest with him about who she was. But even as the thought formed, she knew it was a dangerous idea. There was no point in telling him, except to bring them closer.

If she confessed, then they'd share a secret. He might not be comfortable with that. And there was a small chance he'd give her away and compromise her security. The smart move, the practical move, was to keep it to herself for a couple more days and then quietly go home.

Storm barked.

Sam looked past her. "I can't believe I forgot about him."

Jasmine turned to see the foamy dog standing forlornly in the middle of the garage.

"We have to get him rinsed."

Sam stepped back, but kept his hands on her shoulders. "Thank you for this, Jasmine."

"For bathing Storm?" Or was he thanking her for the kiss?

"For understanding. For being here. For being you." He stroked the backs of his fingers softly over her cheek.

She felt warmed to her soul. "I'm happy to be here, Sam."

She truly was.

Sam woke up happy. It was a strange feeling, a marked difference from every day for the past two years.

He opened his eyes to see the sky was blue and the sun was streaming into his bedroom. The snowstorm had obviously changed course. Or maybe it had disappeared altogether. He'd hoped so, for the sake of everyone along the eastern seaboard. They'd had enough bad weather to last the rest of the holiday season.

Storm was asleep on the floor. He'd parked himself in front of Sam's closed bedroom door last night and stayed there all night long.

Sam sat up and his movement woke the dog.

"I suppose you'll need to go outside right away."

Storm came to his feet and stretched, yawning wide. The dog didn't look like he was in a hurry to do anything, but Sam wasn't taking any chances. He pulled on a pair of comfortable jeans and threw a t-shirt over his head. If he'd had a leash, he would have taken the dog for a walk. But the back yard was fenced, so Storm could go out on his own.

Leaving the bedroom, Sam's thoughts turned to Jasmine. After their kiss, she'd taken everything in stride last night, helping recapture Storm, good-naturedly rinsing and drying him. By now she'd had time to think about it, and he couldn't help wondering how she felt.

He'd sure been thinking about their kiss all night long. He didn't regret it. He'd tried to regret it, but regret was the last thing he was feeling.

Anticipation was what he was feeling. The anticipation that, despite their mutual pledge and despite all the good reasons to stay away from each other, they might just do it again.

"What do you think?" he asked the dog as he pulled on a pair of socks. "Am I losing my mind?"

Storm wagged his tail.

"Is that a yes?"

The dog wagged harder.

Sam heaved a deep sigh. "It's a yes. And you're right. I have no business desiring Jasmine." He came to his feet. "Let's get you outside."

Hearing the word outside, Storm perked up.

"Right. Now that I mention it..." Sam joked. "It's a good idea, isn't it?"

He opened the bedroom door, and the two padded along the hall and down the stairs. Belle was up, making coffee in the kitchen. She wrinkled her nose when she saw Storm.

"He's all clean," Sam assured her.

"I heard a lot of commotion last night," Belle said taking two coffee mugs from the cupboard and setting them on the breakfast bar.

"It wasn't the easiest operation in the world."

"The phones are still working." Her hint was obvious.

Sam moved to the sliding glass door and opened it for Storm. The dog hesitated for a moment then leaped in the deep snow, gamely making his way toward the deck stairs.

"I'll make some calls," Sam said. "See if I can find his owners."

Sam had mixed emotions about sending Storm back to his owners. He knew it didn't make sense to keep the dog, and somebody out there had to be missing him. But he liked the animal, and the girls were wild about the idea of having a pet. He found he wanted to give them that small thing.

Maybe after Christmas they could look at getting a puppy. Belle wouldn't allow it here. But he knew it was time for them to move home anyway. He'd finish the millwork, get the kitchen up and running, and they could do the rest of the renovations while they lived there.

It would be easier anyway, no more commuting back and forth. Melanie had offered to watch the girls after school, and he knew the girls would love to spend more time with Libby.

As the plan came together in his mind, he liked it better and better.

He caught a movement in the corner of his eye, and immediately knew it was Jasmine.

"Good morning." She came in from the living room.

She was dressed in a pair of sleek, black pants and a fitted white blouse. Her hair was loose and soft, slightly wavy and resting on her shoulders. Her face was even more beautiful than he remembered, and he was immediately flooded by a wave of desire.

"Good morning," Belle responded, making Sam realize he'd been staring at Jasmine in dim-witted silence.

"Hi." He managed.

Jasmine smiled at him, and his heart rate spiked.

"Coffee?" Belle asked.

"Yes, please," Jasmine said.

"Sure." Sam spoke right over her.

Belle gave him a look of disbelief. "Well, I knew you were having coffee."

"Thanks," he muttered.

"What's wrong with you?"

"Nothing."

Fortunately for Sam, Storm chose that moment to whimper at the door. He distracted himself by letting the dog back inside.

The girls rushed into the kitchen.

"He's still here," Sophie cried, sliding to her knees and all but careening into Storm.

"Be careful," Sam warned.

"Of course he's still here," Amelia stated with authority. "What are we giving him for breakfast?"

"He ate all the burgers last night," Belle said.

"Bacon?" Sam suggested.

"At five dollars a pound?" Belle was clearly not amused.

Amelia swung open the fridge. "We have baloney."

"I suppose," Belle said.

Sam caught a glimpse of the twinkle in Jasmine's green

eyes. He paused and smiled at her. She smiled in return. It was all he could do to drag his attention away.

Amelia opened a drawer in the refrigerator and retrieved a package of sliced baloney.

"I'll get the water," Sophie offered.

"Your father has some phone calls to make," Belle said.

Sam took his cup of coffee and headed for a quieter spot in the living room.

The route took him right past Jasmine, and despite his better instincts, he paused.

"Sleep well?" he asked.

She nodded. "You?"

"Very well."

He wanted to say more. He wanted to touch her. He was dying to pull her into his arms and hold her there for a long, long time. The strength of his longing rocked him to the core.

"I'll go make those calls." He forced himself to move on.

He heard her talking to Belle from behind him. "Can I help with the pancakes?"

"He's eating," Amelia called out.

"Good boy, Storm," Sophie said.

Sam loved seeing his daughters so happy.

He settled on a sofa in front of the picture window, dialing the local radio station to see if anyone had reported a missing dog.

There was no report there. So he tried the local paper's

office. When they had nothing, he tried the local animal shelter. But nobody had been looking for Storm.

Sam sat back to regroup, letting the chatter from the kitchen wash over him. He supposed going house to house in the neighborhood was his next step. While he was out, he could pick up a collar and a leash. He should probably pick up some dog food as well—just a small bag to see them through.

Amelia joined him, climbing onto the sofa beside him.

"Is Storm leaving now?" she asked, her voice hesitant.

"Not yet," he said.

She smiled and relaxed, leaning against him.

He put an arm around her. "I have to keep looking for his owners."

"Sophie likes him."

"Does she now?" Sam knew that when something was important to Amelia, she always went after it on behalf of Sophie. It was as if she wouldn't admit to any desires of her own.

"She always wanted a dog."

"And what about you?"

Amelia shrugged. "I think Storm needs a good home."

"So we should keep him for his own good?"

Her eyes went wide. "Can we keep him?"

Sam immediately realized what he'd done. "I'm sure somebody out there is looking for him. They must miss him."

"He's a very good dog."

"He does seem to be a very good dog."

Just then, Storm padded in. He plopped himself on the floor next to Sam's feet.

Belle appeared in the doorway. "On my white carpet? Really?"

"He wants to be with Sam," Jasmine said, coming into the room. "He knows the alpha of the pack when he sees him."

"What's an alpha?" Amelia asked.

"The leader," Jasmine answered. Then she held out her hand to Amelia. "Pancakes are ready."

"I'm hungry." Amelia bounced to her feet. "Are you hungry Alpha Daddy?"

"I'm starving." As he moved, sure enough, Storm stayed with him.

"Alpha man," Jasmine muttered as he passed her.

His heart warmed at the silly nickname. Since everyone had their backs to them, he gave into impulse and touched her hand. It was a gentle stroke, just barely grasping her fingers and pulling away to the tips.

Her face flushed and his stomach bottomed out. It took everything he had to keep walking.

Chapter Eight

S AM'S INSUBSTANTIAL TOUCH stayed with Jasmine in the days that followed while she, Belle, Melanie, and many other Tucker citizens decorated the warehouse, prepared food, and pulled together costumes for the children. It was a challenge to keep Sam in the dark. Luckily, Brock was able to keep him busy working on his house.

Now, she stood in the cavernous warehouse, taking in the twinkling lights, the garlands, trees, Santa's workshop, and the artificial snow surrounding the stage. She couldn't help but smile at using snow as a decoration inside, given all that had fallen outside. The second storm hadn't been anywhere near as severe as the first, and things seemed to be slowly getting back to normal. It was five days until Christmas, and the news was reporting a frantic pace across five states as people rushed to get ready.

The first of the guests, those who were helping organize the buffet, trickled in with their costumed children in tow. Belle was home, getting the girls dressed in the silver and lavender dresses they'd chosen for their Christmas princess outfits. They were going to look terrific.

Jasmine knew she had to get back to the house and get dressed herself. Butterflies came up in her stomach as she thought about Sam's reaction to the party. He'd made so much progress on other fronts. And she knew he was happy to see the girls excited about Christmas. She suspected he was still battling some guilt for moving on. But it was obvious he was ready to embrace a band new life.

In her wilder moments of fantasy, she pretended she could be a part of that new life. But the idea was beyond foolish. If he was ready, once he was ready, he'd find a nice girl here in Maine who would be a great mother for Amelia and Sophie. She trusted him to do that. She knew how much he loved his daughters.

She caught a glimpse of Melanie coming toward her and turned to look. Melanie's phone was to her ear. "I'll send Jasmine."

"Send me where?"

Melanie ended the call. "Sam's being stubborn. Brock can't get him to leave the house. He insists he's going to keep working until late tonight."

Their plan had been for Brock to take Sam out for a beer then stop at the warehouse and bring him inside.

"He's been working hard like that for days," Jasmine said.

He'd been coming home late and exhausted every night. His behavior helped keep the party a secret, but she had to admit, she missed talking with him.

"Brock tried to tell him it's time for a break."

"What are we going to do?" Jasmine asked.

"You'll be able to get him here."

"Me?" Jasmine didn't think she was the best choice. If anything, Sam had been avoiding her the past few days. "Maybe Belle should—"

"You're the one who can make him listen," Melanie said.

"No, I can't."

Melanie gave a knowing smile. "Haven't we had this conversation before? I've seen the way he looks at you. Brock's seen the way he looks at you."

Jasmine realized there was no point in pretending it wasn't happening. "He doesn't like it."

"Of course he doesn't like it. His feelings for you are a threat to his grief. He's afraid that if he gives up grieving, he'll lose Kara's memory."

"He won't."

"I know that, and you know that, but Sam can't accept it yet."

"There's nothing going on between us," Jasmine said.

Melanie looked at her strangely. "I never thought there was." Then she looked more closely. "Wait a minute. Did something happen?"

Jasmine couldn't bring herself to lie. "He kissed me. Once. That's all."

"He kissed you."

"It just, kind of, happened."

"That's fantastic."

"It was a mistake. We both regretted it."

"It wasn't a mistake. It was inevitable. And I'm glad it was you. He's coming back to life, and you're helping him. Now, go get him, and bring him to this party. His daughters are counting on him."

"What am I going to say?"

"Get creative. Brock is going to meet you outside and take you to the house."

"Now?"

"Yes, now."

"I have to get dressed." Jasmine looked down at her sweaty t-shirt and dusty jeans. She'd been planning a quick shower and doing something with her hair.

"That'll have to wait. Sam needs you. The girls need you."

Jasmine realized it was true. Amelia and Sophie were counting on their father coming to the party. They were convinced he'd like it. And they'd talked themselves into believing it would change their lives.

Jasmine realized she believed that, too. He was so close. This might be the final push he needed to move on with his life. She realized it would be with someone else. But she couldn't think about that right now. The girls needed her. Sam needed her. And she was going to come through for them all.

She retrieved her jacket and made her way to the front

parking lot, seeing Brock's pickup truck pull up, its headlights bouncing off the bright snowdrifts.

She opened the passenger door and climbed in, taking the briefest of moments to appreciate the normalcy of taking care of herself. Back home, a chauffeur, a security guard, and a doorman would all have helped her inside. And it wouldn't have been a pickup truck. They'd have helped her into a limousine.

"How are things looking in there?" Brock asked as they pulled away.

"It looks fantastic. I can't believe how fast it came together."

"That's the way Tucker does things."

During her short time here, Jasmine had come to appreciate how the town pulled together, worked hard, and supported each other. "You live in a wonderful community."

"I know I do," Brock said. "I appreciate it every day."

They both fell silent for the short drive.

"Any tips?" she asked as they pulled into Sam's driveway.

"He likes you," said Brock, angling his body to look her way.

"I know," she admitted. "I like him, too."

"You're good for him."

"I'll be gone soon."

"You can't stay?"

She shook her head. "I can't stay."

"You're sure."

"I'm positive."

Brock drew a sigh. "That's too bad. For Sam, for you, for everyone."

The conversation made her uncomfortable. It made her foolish fantasies seem more real, and it made her want things that couldn't be. For some reason, her throat grew raw.

"It's impossible," she said in a pained voice.

"I'm sorry to hear that."

Jasmine reached for the door handle, feeling swamped with guilt, feeling as though she was letting Sam, Brock, and everyone else down.

She knocked on the door then rang the bell. When Sam didn't answer, she opened the door. She knew his power tools were loud, and he often wore hearing protection when he was working.

She called his name. When he didn't answer, she mounted the stairs, listening for sounds of work. The house was strangely silent.

She finally found him in the master bedroom. It was quiet, because he wasn't working. He was sitting on the floor, his back against the wall where he'd punched it through, the room completely empty around him. The furniture was gone. The pictures were gone. The curtain rods were bare, even the carpet had been pulled up.

She stopped in the open doorway. "Sam?"

He looked up.

"Are you alright?" She moved slowly into the room, trying to gauge his expression.

He didn't look upset. He looked bemused. But he didn't answer her.

She slid down the wall to sit beside him, waiting, letting him take the lead in the conversation.

"I thought I'd start fresh," he said.

She looked around at the bare walls and the raw wood of the floor. "It looks like you're ready to do just that."

"I gave most of it to goodwill."

"Did Brock know you were doing this?" Jasmine couldn't decide if this was a good sign or a bad sign.

"I never liked the carpet. The curtains were too frilly. And the bed was too small."

"You're getting a new bed?"

"I'm taking down this wall to make more room to fit it in." He tapped behind him. "That part was Brock's idea. I'll put in a steam shower. I really like steam showers."

"You deserve a steam shower."

"I can get everything at wholesale. It'll take a few weeks to do the work. But I usually have a slightly slower season after Christmas, so the timing is good."

"This seems like a good idea."

He came to his feet. "It is a good idea. I haven't had focus for a long time. I'm getting it back, and it feels good."

He held out his hand to her.

She took it, and he helped her rise.

"I'm happy that you're feeling better," she said.

She knew she should let go of his hand, but it felt so good to hold it. She was nearly overcome with a desire to lean into his arms. She wanted to kiss him all over again. She wanted to forget who she was and what her future held and pretend for a moment that she could stay here with Sam and help him redo his bedroom, restart his life.

But she also knew fantasizing that way would only make her real future seem bleak. She had to be strong.

"Do you think we could go somewhere?" she asked, telling herself to focus on the party.

He looked intrigued. "Go where?"

"Maybe a coffee shop for a little while? Most of the shops on Main Street have reopened. I'd like to see some more of Tucker."

"Okay." He gave her hand a brief squeeze. "I could use a break."

"You've been working really hard."

"I've been trying to keep my priorities straight."

"Amelia and Sophie?" She guessed.

"They're number one. Well number one and number two."

It was good to hear him chuckle.

"Can we go to the Lavender Cafe?" she asked.

"Sure." He kept hold of her hand as they walked from the room.

Jasmine knew the route to the Lavender Cafe would take them within a block of the warehouse. It was the best she could do right now. She'd have to come up with a plan along the way to make him turn down the street and go into the parking lot.

SAM DIDN'T KNOW what to make of Jasmine's unexpected invitation. For the past few days, he'd been avoiding her, trying to be respectful of her wishes. She'd been clear she was in no position to get involved with a guy like him.

He knew it was too soon for him. But his core instinct was to stay as close to her as possible. Ready or not, he was falling fast. He couldn't seem to stop himself, and a reckless part of him wanted to give in and hang on for the ride.

So, for now, if she wanted to talk, if she wanted to spend time alone with him, if she wanted what amounted to a date, he was more than willing.

They drove along Main, covering the blocks to the Lavender Café.

"What's going on down there?" she interrupted his thoughts, gesturing down Peak Street.

He swiftly glanced over his shoulder.

As the scene registered, he stomped on the brakes. "What on earth?"

The parking lot of his empty warehouse was full of vehicles parked side by side. His truck slide to a stop on the snowy street, and he pushed the shifter into reverse, backing up to the corner where he could see.

The scene looked unsettlingly familiar. It looked just like it always had for the Christmas party. Then the date hit him in a blinding flash. It was Wednesday, the Wednesday before Christmas.

His hands clenched on the steering wheel, every fiber of his being protesting what was unfolding in front of him.

"They didn't." He rasped out loud. "They *wouldn't*."

"Sam?" There was something in the sound of Jasmine's voice, a hesitation, a hint of guilt, a trace of worry.

He turned to look at her. As he took in her expression, reality hit him like a lightning bolt. "You *knew*?"

"Please don't be angry."

"You think I'm angry?"

He was beyond angry. He was raw with pain. He'd come so far, made so much progress. He'd let down his guard and let her in.

"Everyone's really excited," she said.

"Excited to *celebrate Kara's death*?" Because that's what it felt like to him.

Jasmine looked horrified. "*No*."

"Is this why you came to see me tonight? Is this what you wanted? To drag me to some farce of a party?"

She gaped at him in shocked silence. She swallowed. "I don't think you understand."

"You're the one who doesn't understand."

He was finally getting over the raw pain of killing Kara. He was finally getting to a place where he could ignore, or at least pretend to ignore the mistake that would rightly haunt him for the rest of his life.

"At least come in for a minute. See what they've done. I think you'll appreciate—"

"You think? You *think*? You don't even know me."

She went silent again and the hurt in her eyes nearly crushed his soul.

But he couldn't help that. He couldn't fix that. He had to get far away from the party and far, far away from Jasmine."

"Get out," he told her.

She blinked at him in what looked like pure shock.

"Get out of my truck," he repeated. "Go to the party. Have a great time. But don't ever include me in any of your plans again."

"This isn't about me," she said.

"I know. It's about me."

He pulled the truck into a U-turn.

"Sam!" She protested. "It's about the girls. Can't you at least come in and for a few minutes?"

"You want me to attend the Christmas party where my wife was killed."

The blood drained from Jasmine's face. "Kara was killed at the party?"

"On the way home." He did not want to have this conversation. He wasn't going to have this conversation. "Please get out of my truck."

She gripped the dashboard, facing him. "I didn't know."

"Well, now you do." He wasn't angry anymore. He was tired, dead tired.

"Belle thought you were ready."

"It's not her decision, and it's definitely not your decision."

"You're right, Sam. I apologize." Jasmine seemed genuinely contrite. "You are none of my business. Your family is none of my business. I've obviously done more harm than good here."

He told himself she was getting it. He told himself he was glad she was getting it.

She released her seatbelt and opened the door. "I'll tell Belle we made a mistake."

Jasmine left the truck and firmly shut the door. She started up the road to the warehouse.

Sam drove. He didn't let himself look in the rearview mirror.

He was on Main Street before his heart rate slowed.

He was halfway through town before the fog lifted from his brain and he had the presence of mind to pull over.

He had to face his true feelings.

Jasmine hadn't done a single thing wrong. He was angry with himself not with her. His reaction wasn't about Kara, and it wasn't about the party. It was disappointment about the date with Jasmine at the Lavender Cafe.

This was all about Jasmine. Everything was about Jasmine. She'd come to mean far too much to him.

As soon as she walked into the party, Jasmine knew something was wrong.

The room was too quiet, almost eerily still. There was a large crowd, but the band wasn't playing, nobody was visiting Santa or the buffet, and people were talking to each other in hushed voices.

Glancing around, she realized the problem.

Amelia and Sophie had asked to include photographs of their mother as part of the decorations. It had seemed like a good idea, an homage to Kara. But the pictures were larger than expected, and combined with spot lighting, Kara's presence was very impactful.

Amelia and Sophie were holding hands, pressed together. Belle looked overwhelmed. Nobody seemed to know how to react.

Jasmine didn't know what to do either. But she had to try. She knew she had to help the family who had been so kind to her.

There was a microphone on the stage in front of the band. She had no idea what she was going to say, but she made her way to it anyway, hoping against hope some words would come to her while she walked.

She mounted the short staircase. She could feel all the gazes in the room on her. The crowd grew quieter still and each step felt like an eternity.

She touched the microphone, angling it toward her as Darren had taught her so many times. She knew how close to stand, and she knew how to position her head and her body for an address. Everything Darren had said to her over the years came flooding back. She knew she had to project confidence in order to make the audience feel at ease.

"Good evening, everyone." She kept her tone positive but not too cheerful. She had to respect their discomfort but somehow turn the fragile mood into something positive.

"My name is Jasmine Arcelus. As most of you know, I've only been in Tucker for a short time. While here, I've had the absolute privilege of being hosted by Belle Zachary and her wonderful family. I've gotten to know Amelia and Sophie, and Sam. And through them…" She paused and let her gaze move through a number of the photographs of Kara. "I've gotten to know something about Kara Cutler."

Some people in the crowd shifted at the mention of Kara's name. But Jasmine caught a glimpse of Belle and she looked hopeful. She quickly looked to Amelia and Sophie. They were listening carefully, obviously waiting for her to say more.

"I'm sure it will come as no surprise to any of you when I say I've learned Kara was an extraordinary woman. By all accounts, she was a loving mother, full of creativity and a zest for life, who had time for games and fun with her family."

Jasmine found she was able to relax, and she could feel

the audience relax with her. She silently thanked Darren for his advice, and marveled that it actually worked.

She shared some of the stories the girls had told her. She could feel the moment when the last of the tension left the crowd. One of the stories Melanie had shared popped into her brain. It was funny, and people chuckled as she told it. A few sidebar comments and quiet conversations started up around the room. And she could see heads nodding as other people's memories obviously kicked in.

Though it frightened her to do it, she moved on to Sam, talking about his love for Amelia and Sophie, his lasting love and respect for his late wife, and his determination to carry on for their daughters. She talked about the snowball fight, and about Storm, and about the dog bathing mishap.

Before she finished, everyone was laughing, even Belle, and Jasmine knew it was going to be okay. She seized the moment, inviting the band to start playing and pointing out the buffet tables, thanking all of the volunteers who'd cooked and decorated to get the party ready.

As she turned to leave the stage, she saw Sam standing near the door. Her footsteps faltered along with her confidence. She had no idea how long he'd been there, and she couldn't read a thing in his expression. She hoped he wasn't angry with her for taking over the room.

She'd been trying to help. She thought she had helped. But she knew from experience, good intentions didn't always count.

He held her gaze and she found she couldn't look away. People smiled and thanked her as she passed. She was polite in her responses, but she barely heard what they'd said. Her stomach churned. Had she upset Sam even further? Made him angrier? Made things worse for him?

He didn't move, and she kept walking until she stopped in front of him.

"I'm sorry," she said, not letting herself hesitate. "I'm sorry for keeping you in the dark, for the party, for not respecting what I knew were your wishes."

"It's not your fault," he said. "None of it is your fault."

"I should have told you."

But he shook his head. Then his gaze moved to the stage where the band was now playing. "You know, I've never been able to look at it that way before."

She didn't understand what he meant.

"All these months," he continued. "These years, I've been focused on how Kara's life ended, and on what we'd lost. I couldn't remember all that she'd given us."

Jasmine didn't know what to say. She was afraid to hope. But, she couldn't help herself. For the first time since she'd met Sam, he looked like he was at peace.

He reached for her hands, taking both in his. "Thank you, Jasmine."

The buzz of conversation in the room took an abrupt rise. Suddenly, Amelia and Sophie were rushing through the crowd toward them.

"Daddy," Amelia called out. She grabbed his hand, one barely managing to slide to a stop beside him.

"Daddy, *look*!" Sophie cried, pointing.

Jasmine looked.

The crowd parted, and her father appeared, surrounded by several bodyguards, and Darren was in step behind him.

Her stomach lurched in astonishment, and she automatically curtsied.

Sam stared at the king in obvious confusion.

"What are you doing?" he asked Jasmine, taking in the curtsy. "Who is this? Do you know him?"

It was obvious to the partygoers that the king was someone important. They pointed at him and talked quickly to one another, obviously speculating about his identity.

"Yes," she answered Sam. "That is my father."

Sam seemed to compare their appearances. "Why did you curtsy?"

There was nothing to do but put all of her cards on the table.

"My father." She repeated. "His Majesty, King Elsworth Arcelus of Vollan."

Sam stared at her in incomprehension.

"You're a princess?" Amelia asked in obvious awe. "A *real* princess?"

"I'm a real princess," Jasmine answered. There was no point in pretending anything else.

Her father stopped in front of her. She was immensely

relieved to see Darren in the company behind him. The king had obviously had a change of heart and re-hired him.

"Princess Jasmine." The King intoned, his displeasure with her obvious.

He took in her jeans and t-shirt, her plain shoes, and her messy hair.

"Your Majesty." She curtsied again.

He looked at Sam.

She made the introductions. "Your Majesty, may I present Sam Cutler. He's been kind enough to host me while I was stranded in Tucker."

The king frowned at Sam.

"My mother-in-law was the official host," Sam said, obviously interpreting the king's frown as a criticism of the impropriety of her staying with a man.

Jasmine didn't interpret the king's frown in that way at all. It would never occur to her father that anyone, man or woman, would treat her with anything but the utmost respect. There was something about Sam that annoyed him, but it wasn't their living arrangement.

"Your Majesty," she continued, hoping to move past it, "these are Sam's daughters Amelia and Sophie. They have also been wonderful hosts to me."

The king glanced to the girls.

They both imitated Jasmine's curtsy, causing her to smile with intense fondness.

"Are you a real king?" Amelia asked.

King Elsworth didn't answer. Amelia had no way of knowing she shouldn't speak to the king unless invited.

Jasmine tried to understand his presence. "Your Majesty, do you have an event in America?"

"I'm in America here to bring you home."

To call that unusual, was the understatement of the decade.

"Darren could have picked me up," Jasmine said.

"Darren was the one who lost you in the first place."

Jasmine looked to Darren, who appeared exceedingly nervous. He obviously expected to be fired again within the hour. It was a reasonable expectation.

"It was my fault, Father."

"We will discuss it later." The king gestured to the door.

His aides quickly aligned themselves for his exit.

"What are you doing?" Amelia demanded, placing herself in front of Jasmine.

The king shot the young girl a look of disapproval.

Sam's arm went around his daughter's shoulders, drawing her protectively close.

"Jasmine can't leave." Amelia protested, oblivious to the undercurrents. "The party's just started."

Jasmine was torn. She couldn't disobey her father, but she hated to walk away from Sam and the girls. She especially hated to walk away from Sam right now. She was thrilled he'd changed his mind and come to the party.

She moved closer to her father, speaking quietly. The

aides backed away, giving them privacy.

"Your Majesty, may I have permission to take a moment to thank my hosts?"

His eyes widened in surprise.

"They were very kind." She rushed on.

"Are you suggesting that I *wait*?"

Jasmine realized that she was. It was entirely against protocol to ask the king to wait on anyone else's convenience. But she couldn't leave without a proper thank you.

"A few moments only." She dared to say.

The king looked askance.

"These are extraordinary circumstances," she said.

"Your Majesty." Darren spoke up.

Jasmine was surprised, and the king was obviously shocked at Darren's impertinence. She could only guess Darren thought he had nothing left to lose.

"I can escort Princess Jasmine to the plane."

"Your Majesty." This time it was the king's private secretary who spoke. "You have a call with the ambassador. Perhaps Princess Jasmine could meet us following the call." The private secretary turned to Jasmine. "It will be thirty minutes."

Jasmine held her breath while the king considered the request.

"Acceptable," he finally said. Then he looked to Darren. "Do not let her out of your sight."

Darren gave a sharp nod of acquiescence.

The king turned strode away.

Jasmine hesitantly looked to Sam.

"I want to believe that was a joke," he said, watching the royal group's progress toward the warehouse exit.

"It wasn't a joke."

Sophie reached out, tentatively touching Jasmine's arm.

Jasmine crouched down and gave her a hug. "Oh, sweetheart. It's still me."

Amelia came into the hug.

"But you're a princess," Sophie said.

"Do you have to go?" asked Amelia.

Jasmine nodded. "I'm afraid I do."

"Sophie will miss you."

Jasmine's throat closed up. "And I'll miss Sophie. And I'll miss you, and Belle, and—" She stopped herself, and her gaze rose to Sam.

His expression was unfathomable as she came to her feet.

Just then Belle arrived.

"What's this I hear?" she asked Jasmine.

"Jasmine is a princess," said Amelia.

"A *real* princess," said Sophie.

"Jasmine is leaving us," said Sam, his tone flat.

"Who were all those people?" Belle asked Jasmine.

"Belle," said Jasmine, drawing her into a hug, "I can't thank you enough for letting me stay with you. My father's here now." She drew back. "He's come to take me home." Her voice caught over the last words.

"*That* was your father?" Belle asked.

"Yes. I'm Princess Jasmine Arcelus of Vollan."

"Well, whoever you are, we're going to miss you," Belle said. "When do you have to leave?"

"She has half an hour," Sam said.

Darren looked down at his watch. Jasmine expected him to correct Sam and note they had twenty-five minutes. There was no way he'd allow her to be one second late.

"Can we talk?" she asked Sam. She had no idea what she was going to say, but it needed to be said alone.

"I'll watch the girls," Belle said. "I brought your dress," she said to Jasmine with a helpless shrug. "But I guess there's no time for that."

"I wish there was," Jasmine said, a fresh sadness engulfing her.

She was leaving Tucker. She didn't want to leave Tucker. She wanted to stay for the party. She wanted to see how Sam was doing in the morning. She wanted to enjoy some more of Belle's pancakes. And she wanted to see how Sam's house turned out after the renovations.

But mostly, mostly she wanted to stay with Sam. She wanted to be part of his life. She knew it was impossible, but she also knew with all her heart that it was true.

"Can we?" she asked Sam.

He took her arm. "This way."

She walked with him in silence. She knew Darren would follow at a distance.

"Am I even allowed to touch the princess?" Sam asked, looking at their linked arms.

She tried to make light. "Only if you're invited."

He let her go.

"You're invited," she told him.

But he didn't take her arm again.

"Though here." He opened a door that led to a small office.

He turned on a light and closed the door behind them. There was a grey metal desk, a pair of bookshelves lined with random binders and textbooks. The old computer and telephone were covered in a layer of dust.

He faced her. "I don't understand. Why didn't you tell me?"

"I couldn't. At first I was worried about security."

"You thought I was a danger to you?"

"No. Not you. Anyone, everyone. This is the first time I've ever been alone."

He seemed to contemplate that.

"And then. Well, afterward. I liked the way you treated me, as if I was just like everyone else. I liked pretending I was normal. You didn't know who I was. You didn't know my father. You didn't know"—she couldn't help but smile—"they'd put you in jail for kissing me."

"Jail?"

"I'm afraid so." She gave into temptation and put the flat of her hand against his chest. She could feel his heartbeat.

His expression seemed to relax a little. "Am I about to be arrested?"

"Not if you don't tell anybody in Vollan."

"Are you going to tell anybody in Vollan?" His gaze went to her lips.

She shook her head. "Your secret is safe with me."

SAM COVERED JASMINE'S hand with his. He didn't know what to do. He didn't know what to think. The memory of their kiss was dangling in the air between them.

Did she want him to kiss her again? Did he dare kiss her again? Her assistant, or her bodyguard, or whoever he was, was standing just outside the shipper's office. He doubted there was any such a thing as extradition to Vollan for unauthorized kissing, but he also didn't want to get Jasmine into any trouble.

"I don't know what to do," he told her honestly.

"I don't either." She smiled, and he knew how badly he was going to miss her.

"Why did you come into my life?" he asked.

"It does seem improbable, doesn't it?"

He took both her hands in his. "I so wish you could stay. I want you in my life."

Her smile faded, and her expression turned wistful. "We always knew I couldn't stay."

It was true. But he'd started to hope it wasn't. He hadn't

understood the magnitude of her commitment to her own country.

"Is there someone back home you have to marry?" he asked.

"Not yet. Someday, yes. I have to have children. I don't have any brothers or sisters, and the monarchy must continue."

Sam let that sink in for a minute. "You'll someday be queen."

"I will."

He thought back over their time together. "I made you bathe a dog."

"I offered to bathe a dog. I like Storm. I like him a lot."

"You were so sweet to the girls." What he was thinking was that she'd been amazing to all of them, especially him. She's listened so patiently. She'd offered advice. She'd forced him to face hard truths.

"I love your girls," she said. A sheen came into her eyes, and she blinked rapidly. "I'm going to miss them so much." She paused. "Maybe, maybe…"

"Don't make promises you can't keep."

"This can't be it," she said, a catch to her voice. "It can't be all there is for us."

He gave into impulse and drew her into his arms. Her body felt so perfect against his. "With all my heart, I wish it wasn't. But you have to go," he whispered.

His chest grew so tight it hurt.

"Sam."

"I know." He hugged her tighter, rocking her against him. "Thank you. Thank you for everything."

"All I did was wash a dog and cook pancakes."

"You know that's not all. That's nowhere near all. You made me feel again. You made me want again." He almost said she'd made him love again. But that wasn't true. That couldn't possibly be true.

She tipped her head to him. "Kiss me, Sam."

He did.

He kissed her like there was no tomorrow. Because, there wasn't. There was no tomorrow for them, nothing in their future, nothing he could cling to in the dark of night. He was empty again. After such a short time of being full, he was empty. Only this time it wasn't Kara he would miss.

Chapter Nine

S AM'S HEART TOOK a second hit in as many days. This time it was with empathy for Amelia and Sophie. Tears trickled down their clouded faces as the car carrying Storm disappeared around the corner of the block. Jasmine's speech at the party had alerted Storm's owner to his whereabouts, and they'd called Belle's house this morning, grateful to find their beloved pet.

They were an elderly couple and Sam could hardly ask them to give away their dog.

"Everyone's gone," Amelia wailed, turning to run back into the house.

Sophie sniffed. "I'm sad, Daddy."

Sam lifted her into his arms for a hug. "I'm sad too, sweetheart."

He could feel himself slipping backward into despondency. But he knew he couldn't allow it. He wouldn't allow it ever again. Jasmine or no Jasmine, he was staying strong for his daughters. He'd made up his mind, and he was firm in his decision.

"How would you like to move back home?"

Sophie drew back to look at him. "You mean to our real house?"

"Yes, I mean to our real house." He knew it was time. "I'm still working on the renovations, so not everything works yet. But, if you—"

"Yes!" She beamed at him, her tears drying up. She threw her arms around his neck and squeezed tight. "We can see Libby again. Every day."

"Melanie has offered to watch you after school. So, yes, you would see Libby every day."

"Amelia. Amelia," Sophie called, wiggling to get out of his arms. She hit the floor and ran back into the house, calling to her sister. "We're going home."

Belle arrived as he closed the front door behind him. She raised her brows at Sam in a silent question.

"The girls and I are going home," he said. "It's time."

She looked satisfied. "I'll miss you. But I think that's a good idea."

Amelia flew down the stairs. "Is it true? Are we *going*? Are we going?"

"It's true," Sam said.

Amelia threw herself into his arms. "Sophie is so happy."

"What about you sweetheart? Are you happy, too?"

Amelia nodded against his chest. "When are we going?"

"When do you want to go?"

"Now," said Amelia.

"Now," Sophie echoed.

"What about Christmas?" He looked doubtfully at Belle. "We don't even have a tree."

"We'll get another one," Amelia said.

"You have to come here for dinner," Belle said.

"And you can come over to our house for breakfast," Sophie replied.

"You want to move today?" Sam thought the idea was crazy, but he was thrilled to see the girls so happy.

"We'll go pack," Amelia said.

"What do you think?" he asked Belle.

"I think you're their father, and you know best."

Sam didn't hesitate. Now that the decision was made, he found himself as anxious as the girls. "I think I should take them home."

The girls whooped in delight, jumping up and down. Then they dashed back up the stairs.

"There are some packing boxes in the basement," Belle said.

"I guess then I'm going to pack."

Before he could move, Belle put a hand on his arm. "I know you're going to miss her."

Sam knew he could handle it. He was strong, and he was staying that way. "I'll be fine. I'm good. I'm better than I ever expected I could be."

"Sam," Belle said.

He looked at her.

"I didn't mean Kara."

It took a minute for the words to sink in. When they did, he was filled with longing and regret. He wasn't over Jasmine. He wasn't anywhere near over Jasmine.

"I'll be fine." He repeated, but this time the words sounded hollow.

"She was a wonderful woman."

"She was never what she pretended to be."

He'd spent the past two days trying to harden his heart. He'd known Jasmine could never be his. She'd been clear about that. But despite himself, he'd begun to hope. He'd begun to hope, because he hadn't known how absolutely unattainable she was.

"She was afraid," Belle said. "She never lied to us."

"She said her father was rich."

"He is," Belle answered reasonably.

"She said it was old family money."

"It was."

"Not in the way she led me to believe."

He wished she'd told him from the beginning. If she had, he never would have allowed himself to fall for her. He'd have kept up his guard, and he wouldn't be dealing with fresh heartbreak on top of everything else.

"You fell in love with her," Belle said.

Sam was about to deny it.

"Don't you dare worry about my feelings," Belle said. "We both loved Kara. But I know Kara is gone. And Jasmine is here."

"Jasmine's not here."

He'd only had her in his life for a split second. But yes, he'd fallen in love with her. And now he had to get over it. Denial wasn't going to help him.

"Yes," he admitted to Belle, "I fell in love with Jasmine. But I won't let it overwhelm me. I'm going to be there for my girls."

Belle gave him a squeeze. "I know you will. You made my daughter very happy. Maybe not Jasmine, but there's every chance you'll make another woman happy sometime in the future."

Sam couldn't even imagine that. Lightning striking twice was one thing. Three times was impossible.

JASMINE FELT STRANGELY out of place in her father's office. She was back in her regular clothes. She'd had assistance with her hair and makeup this morning—as she'd had most mornings since she turned sixteen. But it had never felt odd before. It had never seemed strange to have her breakfast prepared in a distant kitchen, brought to her under silver by a neatly dressed waiter.

She couldn't help but think about Sam, Amelia and Sophie, and about Belle's pancakes. Belle made the greatest pancakes in the world. She'd flipped them straight off the griddle onto Jasmine's plate. They were hot and crispy, tender inside with melted butter and maple syrup.

With the time zone change, they were probably getting up right now, the girls in their colorful nightgowns, Belle at the stove, and Sam, Sam…

Jasmine rose from the leather guest chair and moved across the king's office, gazing out the window across the snowy grounds, the fountain, the gardens, the lake beyond. But it was Sam who filled her vision, dressed in his faded jeans, a tight t-shirt, unshaven with bare feet and a sexy smile. He had such a wonderful smile.

She gave herself a shake. She had to stop fantasizing about him. She was attending a children's Christmas concert this afternoon, followed by a formal dinner with dignitaries from all over Vollan. Tomorrow was Christmas Eve, and the festivities would be nonstop until New Year's Day.

She turned from the window and stared blankly at her father's desktop. It was neat and orderly, as was everything in the palace. She'd never thought about it before, but the second something was moved, a staff member magically showed up to put it right. It was the same in her bedroom and her sitting room. It was the silliest thing, but she missed making her own bed and putting away her own clothes.

She'd even learned how to run a washing machine while she was in Tucker. She doubted her father would be impressed, but she was proud of herself. And she'd bathed a dog. And she'd kissed a man. Boy, had she kissed a man.

Her fingertips moved to her lips, imagining she could still feel Sam's touch.

"Stop it." She warned herself.

The second the words were out of her mouth, she glanced guiltily around the office. There was nobody with her, but she felt self-conscious anyway. She dropped her hand to her side.

On the desktop, a paper caught her eye. It was out of place by about an inch, as if someone had been reading it and hastily put it back. She straightened it.

It was a draft of a royal decree, bold, black type on white paper. Someone had edited it by hand. She guessed that would be one of the lawyers, or maybe her father's private secretary. The words "upon the death of the king" jumped out at her. She couldn't stop herself from reading further.

Surely her father couldn't be sick. He was energetic and happy, well as happy as usual, anyway. He's wasn't a frivolous man. But he still rode horses and walked the hills behind the palace.

She lifted the page. As the words registered, her hand trembled. She dropped into his chair and kept reading.

The door opened. The king strode in. He stopped short when he saw her in his chair.

She leapt guiltily to her feet.

"*Princess Jasmine?*" he demanded, obviously shocked by the stunning breach of protocol.

"Prince Norman?" she asked her father.

"How dare you read my private papers."

"You're naming Prince Norman as your heir."

"No," said the king, striding forward and removing the paper from her hand. "I am not. While you were away, we were exploring a theoretical question."

"The theoretical question of me not becoming queen of Vollan?"

Jasmine had no idea how to feel. She was hurt. She was disappointed. But she was also strangely relieved. It had never occurred to her there would be options to her becoming queen.

"It was while you were missing."

"Did you think I was dead?" Even as she asked the question, she realized that couldn't be it. If she was dead, her father's younger brother, Prince Norman would automatically become heir to the throne. They wouldn't need a legal document to accomplish that.

"We did not think you were dead. Darren had told us what happened at your speech in New York." Her father's expression unexpectedly softened. "You've been struggling for years. It wasn't getting any better. I was worried about you."

His uncharacteristic sympathy left Jasmine speechless.

"But then I saw you in Tucker, on stage at the party," he said. "I watched you speak so eloquently and successfully to that crowd."

"You saw that?" She was beyond surprised that he'd been in the warehouse so long before announcing his presence.

"I did. I watched you prove that you were capable. When

I saw you on that stage, I knew you would be queen. You're ready for your destiny, and this paper will be destroyed." He handed it to the attendant behind him.

"Father," she started haltingly, a wild idea forming in her mind. "How… how did Prince Norman feel about this?"

"He was fully prepared to do his duty."

"But was he happy?"

"I don't see how that is relevant."

"Will he be disappointed that you've changed your mind?" she asked.

"I don't—"

"Father, please. I need to know. Did Prince Norman want to be king?"

"None of that matters anymore."

But it did. It might. It gave Jasmine options she never knew she had.

She knew her cousin Princess Adara wanted to be queen. She'd always told Jasmine she was the luckiest girl in the world. She loved all of the royal duties, from attending ceremonies and cutting ribbons, to interacting with children in hospitals and representing Vollan internationally at diplomatic meetings.

An exciting and terrifying idea was anchoring itself in Jasmine's brain.

She stood tall, squared her shoulders, and walked to the private secretary. She held out her hand for the paper, and he immediately pulled it from the folder and handed it to her.

"Please don't destroy this," she said to her father.

"No one will ever know it existed," he assured her.

"I don't know if I want to be queen." She dared to utter. "I'm sorry, Father, but I might not want to be queen."

His face took on a pink hue. "Don't be absurd."

She held up the paper. "It's possible to change my destiny. You've just shown me it's possible."

"You have proven yourself more than capable. I was wrong to even consider it."

"Something happened in Tucker, Father."

His face went darker, his brows knitting together in what looked like emerging anger. "What did you do?"

"I fell in love." As she said the words, an enormous feeling of lightness came over her entire body. She loved Sam. She loved him so much.

"What did you do?" he repeated.

"Nothing. I talked to him. We washed a dog together."

"A *dog?*"

You'd have thought she said they'd robbed a bank.

"I got to know him. And I kissed him. I love him deeply, and I want so desperately to go back to him."

"You're talking nonsense," the king said with absolute authority.

"It's not nonsense." She loved Sam. And that last day, those last few moments together, she could have sworn he was about to say he loved her. He said he wanted her in his life. And she very much wanted to be in his.

"You cannot marry an American," the king said.

"Is there a law against it?"

HE DIDN'T ANSWER. His jaw clenched tight, and he stared hard into her eyes.

She stood her ground. "Please, Father. Let me go to Sam."

The king's gaze unexpectedly softened. "You love him that much?"

"I do."

"It would be extraordinary."

"It would make me very happy."

"Then I will make him a duke,"

The statement startled Jasmine into silence.

"The Duke of Holden."

"That's not what I meant."

"Maybe not. But that is my offer, daughter. You cannot forsake your kingdom."

"Sam will want to stay in Maine." Jasmine knew how much Sam loved the town of Tucker.

If he loved her, and she desperately hoped he did. He would still be determined to raise his daughters in his home town.

The king leaned forward and gave Jasmine a kiss on the forehead. "If he loves you, he will share your life. Ask him to come to Vollan."

Jasmine wasn't at all certain of that. "If he refuses, I want to stay with him."

"If he refuses, we will talk again."

But Jasmine's mind was already made up. If Sam loved her in return, no matter what it took, she'd find a way for them to be together.

SAM AND THE girl's Christmas tree was a bit sad, hastily put together, and the kitchen was still halfway under construction. Shopping had been curtailed due to the storm, so there were fewer presents than usual. But Christmas morning dawned to two happy little girls.

They'd torn into their presents with apparent gusto, and were now rushing around the house having a mock sword fight with the empty cardboard Christmas wrapping cylinders. Sophie was humoring Amelia, who had promised to make jewelry with Sophie's new kit later on.

Sam was sizing up the supplies in the refrigerator, wondering if he had enough to make pancakes. He could always call Belle and get her to bring along a few things. But he was hoping to pull breakfast off himself. It felt like a small measure of independence.

The doorbell rang, and the girls shrieked in delight, rushing through the living room. It would be Libby, probably still in her pajamas, ready to show off her gifts.

It was such a normal little moment and he was happy for

his girls. Unfortunately, he was incredibly sad for himself. He'd missed Jasmine every minute of every day since she'd left. His heartache was acute, and he couldn't seem to accept the fact that she wasn't coming back.

He heard Libby's voice joining the chorus. The door slammed shut, and the girls rushed off up the stairs.

Sam went back to the fridge, checking the level in the milk carton then opening the freezer to confirm they had blueberries.

The doorbell rang again—probably Brock or Melanie with the boys this time. It looked like he was going to have a make a lot of pancakes.

He made his way through the living room, picking up some stray wrapping paper to help clear the clutter. Then he opened the door.

"I have a—" He stopped. He blinked and shook his head to clear his vision.

But she was still there.

"Jasmine?"

She was smiling. "Merry Christmas, Sam."

"You're—" He looked behind her for bodyguards and attendants that ought to be watching over her. All he saw was a sedan sitting at the curb. "Here?"

"I'm here," she said softly.

"I don't understand."

How could she be here? It was Christmas Day. She was the Crown Princess. She must have a dozen things to do in

Vollan.

It was then he saw movement in her hands.

She was holding a puppy. It was a small, golden ball of fuzz, with floppy ears, big paws, an adorable face and a red bow around its neck.

"Jasmine, Jasmine," Amelia shouted from behind him, and Sam was immediately surrounded by three young girls.

"Oohh, it's a puppy!" cried Sophie. "Jasmine brought us a puppy!"

"Can I hold him? Can I hold him?" Amelia asked.

"Hold him gently," said Jasmine, handing the puppy carefully into Amelia's hands.

Amelia rubbed her face against its fur. "Sophie will love you so much."

The puppy's tail wagged and Sophie scratched his head.

The girls disappeared into the house, while Sam drank in the sight of Jasmine.

She looked directly into his eyes, her own shining with happiness.

"Is that why you came?" he asked, still baffled. "All this way to deliver a puppy?"

He couldn't stop the wild surge of hope that her appearance might mean something more. He needed that hope dashed right away.

"It's an awfully long way to deliver a puppy," she said, stepping forward.

"It is," he agreed, but that didn't answer his question.

He was fighting to keep from touching her.

But then she touched her hands to his and he lost the battle. He pulled her forward, hugging her close, holding her tight.

"Tell me," he whispered into her ear. "Say it. Whatever this is or isn't, just tell me so I can stop hoping."

"I came back to you," she said.

"Why?" He could hear the pain in his own voice, laced with hope, laced with fear.

"To love you, Sam. I came back to love you."

Joy rushed uncontrollably through him. "How is that possible?"

"I had a difficult talk with my father."

"Are you okay? You didn't run away or anything?" He desperately wanted Jasmine, but he didn't want to harm her relationship with her family.

"I didn't run away. I told him you were more important to me than the throne."

Sam drew back in complete shock. "You what?"

"I love you, Sam. And if you feel the same way—"

"I do." He stated emphatically, holding her tight once more. "I love you so much, Jasmine."

"Then we'll figure the rest out."

"You can't give up your country."

"I can, and I will. But there's another option."

He knew what she was saying. The question was there in her eyes. And it was a huge, huge decision.

He didn't know the answer. So he kissed her instead. It was a long and fulfilling kiss. It was everything he remembered, and this time he vowed to make it last forever.

He finally drew back, breathless, grinning into her flushed expression. "We have to talk."

"We do,"

"We'll figure it out," he vowed. "And we'll be together."

Epilogue

THEY'D BROKEN WITH royal tradition to host a winter wedding in Vollan. Sam hadn't wanted to wait, and neither had Jasmine. Amelia and Sophie loved the palace, and the staff seemed to adore the girls. They'd been over the moon at getting fitted for their gowns, and they had been perfect junior bridesmaids.

The ceremony was now over, the flower petals thrown, and the proclamation read to the citizens of Vollan. There'd been a cheer outside the cathedral as Sam and Jasmine emerged and greeted the crowds. Then the entire wedding party rode back to the palace in a line of limousines, where tables had been set for a fifteen course dinner, and a ten tier cake dominated the formal ballroom.

"Welcome to the family," Princess Adara said to Sam, giving him a kiss on the cheek. "Don't take her away too often."

Jasmine saw her father approach. She touched Sam's hand to warn him. She and Adara curtsied, while Sam gave a small bow.

"Your Majesty," Jasmine greeted.

"Congratulations, my darling." He gave her a rare kiss on the cheek.

"And the new Duke of Holden," the king said to Sam.

Jasmine knew Sam was struggling to get used to having a title, but he'd definitely agreed on the choice. Holden was an old title, with woodlands in the south of the country. Sam could grow, cut and mill his own wood. He already had ideas for growing an entire furniture industry.

Amelia and Sophie arrived, laughing with Belle.

When they saw the king, both immediately sobered and curtsied the way they'd been practicing. They were dressed in aqua tulle gowns, and still carried their small bouquets.

"And these two," the king said in a kindly voice, "my brand new granddaughters." His expression was softer than Jasmine had ever seen and he crouched down to talk to the girls.

Jasmine did a double take at his strange behavior. She looked to Adara, whose eyes had widened as well.

"You're members of the royal household now," he told Amelia and Sophie.

The girls were in obvious awe. Amelia took Sophie's hand.

"Your father will be a duke in Vollan, and your mother is a royal princess. Do you know what that means?"

Both girls shook their heads.

The king motioned to an aide, who came forward with a purple velvet cushion in hand.

"That means," the king said, slowly drawing his ceremonial sword, "that I have to make you princesses."

The girls' eyes went enormously wide, and then they both grinned ear to ear.

The king held his sword between them and spoke solemnly. "Do you pledge allegiance to the king and the people of Vollan?"

"Yes." Sophie managed.

Amelia could only nod.

The aide lowered the cushion, and the girls saw the two matching diamond tiaras.

They both gasped.

As the king placed them on their heads, Sam leaned close to Jasmine's ear. "Did you know he was going to do this?"

"I didn't. He's really taken a shine to your daughters."

Sam sounded worried. "I don't know how we're going to keep them grounded."

"We'll visit Tucker. We'll visit a lot. And I'll help you raise them. I've been a little princess, and I remember what it's like."

"And you grew up beautifully," Sam said, putting his arms around her. "I adore you Princess Jasmine."

She leaned into his embrace. "I adore you right back, Duke Holden." There was a thread of laughter in his voice. "Oh, yeah that's going to take a while."

"You'll get used to it."

His voice was deep and definitive. "For you, I'll get used to anything. We're truly going to make this work, aren't we."

"We truly are."

The End

If you enjoyed *His Jingle Bell Princess*, don't miss Barbara Dunlop's new series...

The Match series

The comedic, contemporary romance series featuring the high-tech antics of matchmaking senior citizens unleashed on their unsuspecting heirs

Book 1: *An Unlikely Match*
Book 2: *An Impractical Match*
Book 3: *An Extraordinary Match*
Book 4: *An Astonishing Match*
Book 5: *An Unpredictable Match*

Get swept away for a sweet royal holiday...

His Jingle Bell Princess by Barbara Dunlop
A Royal Christmas Princess by Scarlet Wilson
Christmas at the Castle by Melissa McClone

Available now at your favorite online retailer!

About the Author

Barbara Dunlop is a New York Times and USA Today bestselling author of fifty romance novels. A three time finalist in the prestigious RITA award, she is also a two time winner of the RWA Golden Heart award. An Unlikely Match, the first book in her acclaimed Match series, was a number one bestseller on Amazon. Barbara makes her home in Yukon with her bush pilot husband and the moose and bears that wander through their yard.

Visit Barbara at BarbaraDunlop.com

Thank you for reading

His Jingle Bell Princess

If you enjoyed this book, you can find more from all our great authors at TulePublishing.com, or from your favorite online retailer.

TULE
PUBLISHING